He didn't kiss █████████

and Esther didn't exp████████
leaned against the doo████████
emotions of the eveni█████████ her. Healing, she
thought. There was a matter of healing she needed to
remember. Esther was the fix-it lady—whatever a
person's ills, she had a need to try to soothe them.

And if ever a man needed the healing of a loving
woman, Alexander Stone did. Trouble was, not all
healing took. Her real task, she decided, was to raise
her two children into healthy adults. She couldn't
allow any man to interfere with that. But as she started
a bath and then slipped into the warm, lavender-
scented water, Esther felt again the heavy thudding
of her heart that Alexander's kiss had aroused, and
she knew she'd be hard put to resist him....

Dear Reader,

Welcome to Silhouette **Special Edition** . . . welcome to romance. Each month, Silhouette **Special Edition** publishes six novels with you in mind—stories of love and life, tales that you can identify with—romance with that little ''something special'' added in.

May has some wonderful stories blossoming for you. Don't miss Debbie Macomber's continuing series, THOSE MANNING MEN. This month, we're pleased to present *Stand-in Wife,* Paul and Leah's story. And starting this month is Myrna Temte's new series, COWBOY COUNTRY. *For Pete's Sake* is set in Wyoming and should delight anyone who enjoys the classic ranch story.

Rounding out this month are more stories by some of your favorite authors: Lisa Jackson, Ruth Wind, Andrea Edwards. And say hello to Kari Sutherland. Her debut book, *Wish on the Moon,* is also coming your way this month.

In each Silhouette **Special Edition** novel, we're dedicated to bringing you the romances that you dream about—stories that will delight as well as bring a tear to the eye. And that's what Silhouette **Special Edition** is all about—special books by special authors for special readers!

I hope you enjoy this book and all of the stories to come!

Sincerely,

Tara Gavin
Senior Editor
Silhouette Books

RUTH WIND
A Minute To Smile

 Silhouette Special Edition

Published by Silhouette Books New York

America's Publisher of Contemporary Romance

For Ram, the fierce and tender lion who is my husband

SILHOUETTE BOOKS
300 East 42nd St., New York, N.Y. 10017

A MINUTE TO SMILE

ISBN: 0-373-09742-5

First Silhouette Books printing May 1992

Printed in the U.S.A.

Books by Ruth Wind

Silhouette Special Edition

Strangers on a Train #555
Summer's Freedom #588
Light of Day #635
A Minute To Smile #742

RUTH WIND

has been addicted to books and stories for as long as she can remember. When she realized at the age of seven that some lucky people actually spent their days spinning tales for others, she knew she had found her calling. The direction of that calling was decided when the incurable romantic fell in love with the films *Dr. Zhivago* and *Romeo and Juliet*.

The Colorado native holds a bachelor's degree in journalism and lives with her husband and two young sons at the foot of the Rockies.

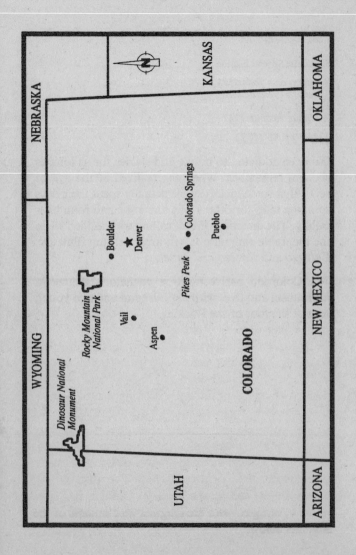

Prologue

From the window seat in his tiny office, Alexander Stone could see a great portion of the university campus. The big, multipaned window was the one redeeming feature of the stuffy room, located high in a tower, and today the view acted as a balm on his aching heart. Trees branched out in feathery green, waving their slender topmost branches into a vivid Colorado sky. Beyond the sprawling campus, dusty blue foothills surrounded the city of Boulder like brawny sentinels.

Alexander's gaze was focused below, upon the whirling reds and russets and wines of a festival sponsored by the history club each year. The sound of medieval flutes and harps floated through his open window, mingled with the laughter and catcalls of the students below.

He watched the quadrangle for a long time. As usual, everyone had thrown themselves into the preparations for the fair—a great many of them his students. He had been among them until an hour ago, when the sense of his own isolation had driven him upstairs to this quiet room. Once, he had enjoyed the bustle and noise, but that had been back in the days when he'd had someone to share it with. Now the fair seemed like just another obligation to fulfill.

Obligations. He eyed the stack of final exams on his desk, but the thought of wading through them held absolutely no appeal.

Picking up a pair of binoculars he kept in the office to examine the birds that often sang outside the window, he scanned the high branches and was rewarded with the sight of a shiny black crow alighting briefly on a branch before it swooped down toward a knot of discarded food on the sidewalk. Alexander watched the bird descend almost dizzily, snag the food and sail away.

Through the binoculars, he caught sight of a group of his students who were singing a rousing—and no doubt bawdy—song in front of a hedge. He smiled to himself. Farther on was a fellow professor, sprawled against a tree, eating chicken. A pair of dark-haired children chased one another in the grass. Handsome lads, he thought distractedly, moving his binoculars a little farther.

He paused as a woman came into view, no doubt the mother of the two little boys. The vivid yellow of her blouse caught his eye, a yellow impossibly at odds with the cloud of pale red hair skimming her bared shoulders. Those colors should never have worked together, he thought.

But they did. He admired the bold combination for a moment, and found his eyes sweeping the flawless, milk-white of the woman's skin. Generous breasts and hips balanced the roundness of her arms. As he watched, she laughed robustly, then reached out to snag one of the children, affectionately tumbling him into her lap to nibble his neck and tickle his ribs. There was a vividness about the woman, about the vibrant love spilling out from her that stirred Alexander deeply.

As the small boy giggled helplessly against his mother, Alexander felt a wistfulness move through him, a pinch of hunger he'd not felt in a long time. He watched the woman kiss her child almost reverently, then hold out an arm to the other boy, who sank next to her, his face flushed.

All three of them simply sat there for a moment, spent with the festival, dappled by the speckled shade that fell through the branches of an oak tree. Alexander felt the restless stirring within him grow and ache for an instant before he could push it away. He threw down his glasses and turned away from the window, shedding the mantle he'd worn for the festival in favor of his street clothes. There was no restlessness, no pain that a good round of combat in the dojo couldn't cure.

Chapter One

Esther Lucas was running late. As usual. This afternoon, it was for a typical reason. She'd been unable to find the boys' *gis,* which turned out to be exactly where she'd put them—folded in a neat stack on the dryer. It was the towels folded on top of them that had thrown her off.

Now she checked her watch and hurried the boys along. "Come on, guys. This isn't a city hike. We have to get to the dojo."

"Sensei said it's important to be on time," Jeremy, her youngest reminded her.

"I know." *Sensei said* had preceded a solid third of his sentences in the past few weeks. Most of them were the kinds of things a mother loved to hear her children mouth, but they all mainly revolved around a sense of orderliness and balance that Esther had never mastered.

"We're almost there," she said. "See?" She pointed to a small, unassuming building sandwiched between a photographer's studio and a quilting shop. A sign in the window announced the form taught, shokatan karate, and the instructor's name, Ryohe Kobayashi, in Roman letters. The lovely calligraphy of Japan followed, presumably announcing the same information.

The boys slowed as they reached the door and entered the dojo with a dignity and hush that always surprised her. Esther tagged behind, scowling at the bank of heavy clouds that hung over the mountains. Ordinarily the precious hour the children spent at their lessons was the only time she had to herself in a day. She used it to stroll along the streets nearby, sometimes stopping for a cup of tea or a sweet while she waited.

Today, the impending rain made that impossible.

Just inside the doors of the studio was a bank of chairs and Esther settled in one, desultorily taking out a book to read while she waited, thinking with longing of the piece of pie she'd intended to treat herself to before the clouds had ruined her plan.

A pretty Asian girl sat behind a low counter to Esther's right, tallying numbers on an adding machine. She smiled at Esther's sigh.

Off to the left through an archway, was the main room. Long and wide, it consumed the rest of the space in the dojo except for a few smaller rooms toward the back.

Her wandering gaze caught on the figure of a man at her end of the dojo going through elaborate, stylized exercises. It was tai chi, Esther realized after a moment; the same form her friend Abe practiced.

But Abe had never looked like this.

The man wore only a loose pair of trousers, leaving his chest and feet bare. Tall and lean, with thick, unruly dark hair and a beard, his movements sent the long muscles in his arms and back rippling with the sleek grace of a jungle cat. His skin was tawny, his nose blunt and broad, and his hair curled over his well-shaped head like a mane.

A mane, Esther thought. Yes. He was no ordinary jungle cat. A quickening shivered through her middle. He looked like a lion—king of all the lesser beasts, master of jaguars and tigers and foolish monkeys. It was in the arrogant tilt of his proud head, in the intelligence of his wide brow.

The quickening rippled outward from her belly, into her limbs. Who was he? She knew she had never seen him here before.

As he shifted once more, the light from a window high on the wall spilled over him, showing tiny strands of silver in the glossy mahogany hair. He wore a neatly trimmed beard, and it had been heavily painted with the same silver. Esther inclined her head with a small frown, sure he'd not yet seen forty. She wondered if genetics or tragedy had given him that early frost.

Absently she thought she should quit staring. But somehow it seemed as silly to turn her eyes away from the natural splendor of his male form as it would be to turn away from the brawny shoulders of the mountains. She let herself admire him until his set was complete. He paused, shaking his hands loosely. The heavy canvas trousers rode his hipbones, showing a lean, tanned stomach with a line of dark hair running over the muscles as if for emphasis. Another quiver ran over her nerves.

Then he met her gaze and for an instant, she was riveted. It was an unflinchingly masculine face, rendered in clean, bold strokes. But she was snared less by the face itself than by something strangely compelling in his unsmiling expression. There was incandescence in his eyes, and a definite sense of recognition.

As she watched, a strange flash of bleakness bled everything else from his eyes, giving Esther a fleeting glimpse of a hopelessness so vast she could barely fathom it.

Abruptly he bent down to pick up a short canvas robe. As he walked toward the back of the room, carefully skirting the mat where the children were practicing, he shrugged into the robe. He didn't look back.

Esther touched her breastbone, feeling her heart threading below. A blast of rain struck the window behind her and she started, whirling to look at the gray sheeting into the glass. The bleakness in the man's eyes had looked just that color, she thought, and decided that tragedy had silvered his beard.

Several days later, Esther washed shelves in the organic and natural foods shop she ran from the front of her old home. The alternative radio station was playing a Jelly Roll Morton tune and the fragrance of a freshly brewed pot of her special herb tea wafted through the sunny, plant-filled room. Expertly she analyzed the scent as she dusted antique tins that held plastic bags of the same mixture of rose hips, hibiscus, chamomile and various other beneficial herbs.

"Too much hibiscus this time," she told the Victorian face on the ornate box.

The bell over the door rang and Abe Smith limped in. "Caught you talking to your tins again," he teased with a shake of his head.

Esther grinned ruefully. "You always do." She watched him carefully, a tall man with thick dark hair he wore too long and the remains of an acne-ravaged childhood on his face. He moved stiffly, each step carefully measured. "Bad day?" she asked gently.

"Yeah," he agreed. "I need some of that bath stuff you make for me."

"Well, you just sit yourself down. I'll make you a cup of tea to drink while you wait."

"Real sugar."

"No problem." She shot him an amused glance. The two of them shared a love of white sugar, although Esther tolerated honey in her tea when purists were shopping. "I've got some glazed doughnuts in the kitchen if you want one," she added in a conspiratorial tone.

He shook his head. "Not today, thanks."

When he settled with his tea, she measured herbs for his bath preparation. In spite of the fact that she'd found the recipe in a sixteenth-century text on herbal lore, it was hardly an exotic mixture—ordinary garden herbs.

"Where's Jeremy?" Abe asked, sipping his tea.

"Outside, no doubt killing dragons or scaling mountains or slaying the enemy with his superior brand of martial arts."

"What a kid."

"Right," Esther replied dryly. "What a kid. He's a daredevil with all the caution of a kamakazi."

"But he's got a great imagination."

"Sure. All I have to do as a mother is see that he makes it to adulthood in one piece so that he can do something with that imagination." She rolled her eyes. "I have my doubts some days."

Abe wiggled his nose, a sure indication he was about to tease her. "Great soldier material."

"Not if I can help it," she replied firmly and frowned at him. "Honestly, how can you even tease me about that?" He was so full of shrapnel he could barely walk some days.

"Once a Marine, always a Marine." He lifted a heavy eyebrow, amusement in his dark eyes. "And unlike soldier boy out there in the backyard, for me it was all in pursuit of the admiration of women." His nose wiggled again. "It worked for all the guys in the movies."

She gave him the sealed plastic bag of herbs. "Good thing the good Lord invented women," she said with a wry smile. "Otherwise, who would heal you?"

"We'd figure something out," he said.

Esther grinned. They'd met when Esther was eight, Abe almost thirteen, and had been friends ever since. "How are you, really?"

"I'm okay, Mom. Just a little stiff."

"All right. I'm going to go check on Jeremy, then."

But as she was turning toward the back of the house, the bell rang over the door. For an instant, she listened to see if she could hear her son's voice. It came to her faintly, full of the undertones of command he used in playing his games. Reassured, she turned to greet her new customer.

Him.

The lion man from the dojo stood just inside the door, looking no less powerful than he had last week.

Instead of loose trousers and bare feet, he wore a hand-tailored cotton shirt, open at the collar, and jeans that fit his lean thighs well. Light from the windows haloed his thick, curly hair and outlined the breadth of his shoulders. In his big, brown hands he held a white Panama hat.

For an instant, all she could do was look at him in surprise, and he seemed as stunned as she. When the silence between them stretched to an almost unbearable length, Esther finally broke it.

"Hello," she said. "Can I help you?"

Abe jumped up. "Esther, this is a friend of mine from the dojo, Alexander Stone."

The man extended his hand. "Hello," he said. "Abe has been telling me about your expertise with herbs." The voice was richly textured, as deep as a summer midnight, the edges and vowels of his words clipped with a British accent. Esther felt it flow over her spine as his strong, callused hand grasped hers firmly.

Rattled, she shot Abe a glance. "He has?"

Alexander dropped her hand. "I've been looking for someone to help teach a summer class. Abe said you're the most knowledgeable herbalist in Boulder."

"He overestimates me," Esther said with a smile. His eyes, she thought, were a very unusual shade of blue—a clear aquamarine that made her think of marbles.

"You've got the right woman," Abe interjected from his seat by the tea table. "Esther is about to be modest and mild, but she's the best there is."

Again she was about to protest, but a single scream pierced the air, cutting through the sound of the radio and their conversation. Without an instant's hesitation, Esther turned and ran for the backyard, her heart pounding in fear. Jeremy was, in addition to being an eccentric little daredevil, very loud, and he was known to shriek in frustration. But the scream she heard had been one of pain and fear.

As she slammed out the back door, she cursed herself inwardly. Her instincts had told her to check on Jeremy a moment ago. She should have listened— they'd proved true more than once. If anything serious had happened to him—

He lay beneath the crab apple tree unmoving, flat on his back. Esther raced toward him and kneeled in the grass. "Jeremy!" she cried.

He opened his eyes and coughed, then promptly burst into tears.

"Are you all right, honey?"

"I fell!" he wailed and sat up to throw himself into his mother's arms. The tears were as much a defense from the wrath of the scolding he knew was coming as in fear.

She hugged him for a moment, then loosened his grip around her neck to look at his face. "How many times have I told you to stay out of that tree?"

"But, Mommy—"

"Not a word, Jeremy. You could have broken your neck." She paused to let the meaning sink in. "You can't watch any television for the rest of the week."

His head dropped, the dark curls tumbling forward in glossy disarray, and his plump lower lip popped out. "Okay," he said in a tragic voice. Then he realized the consequences of his actions. "That means I can't watch Sesame Street!" He wept, and threw himself against her chest again.

For a moment, Esther simply held him in her arms, reveling in the smell of little boy—sunshine in his hair and dust on his clothes. She felt the heat of his wire-taut limbs against her palms and the prickling of his hair against her shoulder. And in memory, she saw him lying so still in the grass.

What was she going to do with this child?

Alexander fingered the tins on the shelf as he waited for Esther to return, and admired a row of jewel-toned jellies with hand-lettered labels: rose petal, choke-cherry, crab apple. Curiously he picked one up. "I've never heard of anything like this," he commented to Abe, who had returned to sipping tea in a rattan chair next to a huge fern.

"You ought to give them a try." He grinned and lowered his voice. "Esther would probably hang me for saying so, but you get the flavor best if you make the toast out of white bread."

Alexander smiled appreciatively, for he was no stranger to the fanatical devotion of many Boulder-ites to natural foods. He lifted the jar toward the light, admiring the pale ruby color. "It's beautiful."

"Esther makes it."

"Do they have healing properties?" Alexander asked with a grin.

"No. But they'll do wonders for your attitude."

Esther breezed back into the room. Once again, Alexander felt himself riveted upon her. Instead of the bright yellow peasant blouse of the festival, she wore a brown rayon dress with buttons up the front. It was oddly old-fashioned, a dress from the forties, and it clung with demure but enticing exactness to her generous curves. "Abe," she said with a toss of wild red hair, "would you mind sitting with Jeremy outside for a few minutes? He's pouting, but he might like a friend."

"Maybe I'll go tell him some soldier stories," Abe said with a wicked grin and headed for the backyard.

Esther turned toward Alexander, brushing wisps of hair from her porcelain face. "Would you like to sit down?" She gestured toward a rattan love seat.

As he settled on floral cushions, he decided that she made him think of a goddess, but not those ethereal creatures artists were so fond of, with their flat blond hair and frail figures. Rather, Esther was more like an ancient goddess of fertility—laughing and lusty, drawn in robust hues, love and appetite flowing from her like sunshine.

Oddly appropriate that she was an herbalist.

"Since you're English, I'm sure my tea won't suit you," she said, "but can I offer you a glass of lemonade?"

Alexander had to gather his scattered thoughts to speak and it annoyed him. He was thirty-nine years old and in addition to having been married twelve years, he was no stranger to women. What was it about this woman that tied his tongue? "Lemonade is fine," he said gruffly.

"Fresh squeezed," she said, sliding open the door of a glass-fronted cooler that displayed all sorts of exotic juices and soft drinks. She poured a tall glass of lemonade for each of them from a pitcher, then settled in the chair Abe had vacated. The pose put her against the light, giving her hair an edging of gold fire. Taking a dainty sip of her lemonade, she gave him a curious glance. "So, tell me more about this class."

Alexander fingered his beard momentarily, gathering his thoughts. "My specialty is the history of the dark and middle ages, and I've several students who need a touch of reality regarding their favorite time period."

She flashed that inviting, mysterious, goddess smile. "How interesting. What would you like me to do?"

"We need someone to share the old ways of medicine with us. Abe said there's no one who knows the herbal arts as well as you do."

Again she brushed away the compliment. "He's much too loyal. But I love talking about herbs on any level." Biting her lip, she paused. "I think I may even have a few books on the dark ages in particular."

"An honorarium would be arranged, of course." He forced himself to look away from the glowing colors of the woman before him and sipped the pulpy lemonade.

"Waive the honorarium," she said. "It's been a while since I've taken a class of any kind. I might enjoy sitting in on the sessions that I don't teach." She looked at him, a hint of shyness in her rich brown eyes. "Would that be all right?"

"Of course." He smiled to put her at ease and cocked an eyebrow. "Does that mean you'll do it?"

"How many students are in the class?"

"Only eleven—most of them very intense, I should warn you. The sort of students that live and breathe for history. All of them are very bright, eloquent, and—" he gave her a rueful smile "—absurdly certain that the world we left was a far better one than the one in which we live."

"You sound as if you know them very well."

"Oh, I do. I proposed the class with all of them in mind. Obsession can be dangerous." He shook his head. "You'll see what I mean soon enough, I'm afraid."

"Believe me," Esther said with asperity, "I'm familiar with the syndrome." She laughed. "I've probably even been one of those students."

"As have I, I'm afraid."

A group of little boys rushed up to the door. "Mrs. Lucas, can Jeremy play?" one called through the screen.

"He's around back, guys."

Alexander watched the gaggle of them run toward a parked group of trikes and tiny two-wheelers.

"Do you have children?" Esther asked.

"No," he said.

"Somehow I didn't think so."

"Oh, really? Why is that?" His question was more curious than anything.

"You strike me as someone with an orderly life—and don't ask me why, because I don't know."

For a moment, he was surprised, then he laughed at how accurately she had pegged him. "As a matter of fact, I do have an orderly life." He inclined his head, realizing with a small part of his mind that it had been literally years since he'd laughed out loud so spontaneously. "But would I still live amidst disorder if my children were grown and gone?"

"Not a chance, Professor. That silver might fool some people, but you aren't old enough to have children already sprung from the nest."

"Right again," he said. He stood up. "I've got a feeling I'm going to like working with you, Ms. Lucas."

She inclined her head, as if taking his measure, a measure that somehow puzzled her. "The feeling is mutual."

"I'll send you a syllabus for the class and you'll have a clear idea of what I'll need from you on that." He stood up and extended a hand. "I'm listed in the university directory if you should have any questions—and I don't live very far from here, either."

"All right. It was nice to meet you, Alexander Stone."

"Goodbye," he said formally, and firmly placed his hat on his head. Outside, the day seemed bursting with life and energy. He decided suddenly to forego the work he'd had planned for this afternoon in favor of working out at the dojo.

As he walked home to get his things, he found himself whistling.

Chapter Two

The dojo was nearly empty on this warm afternoon, which suited Alexander as well as if it had been filled with people. He didn't come here for social reasons.

The room was still, with reflected light falling in soft white arcs to the mats from windows high in the walls. It smelled faintly of hardworking bodies and the polish on the floors, with a hint of the incense Ryohe Kobayashi burned in his private room. As Alexander headed barefooted toward the unoccupied end of the room, he nodded at a young muscular man working with a heavy bag suspended from the ceiling.

Shutting external signals out, Alexander moved into the tai chi chuan exercise that had led him into the practice of martial arts as a boy. A series of 128 slow-motion movements, it served to loosen his body and shut down his brain. After so many years, he was able to block his rational processes, but another portion of his mind never entirely quieted. A purely sensual vision of Esther flashed against the darkened screen of memory, a vision of yellow light shimmering in her pale copper hair, of her sloe-eyed smile and throaty voice.

No thoughts. He pushed them away, slowly easing away even the vision of Esther as he sought the quiet of mind that marked true discipline.

Some days, when he worked hard and long, he found himself suspended in the flow and concentration that marked the art of tai chi. Not often—it was nearly impossible for a Western man to completely master the art of silence. But the mellow sense of peace occurred often enough that he continued to seek it. In the past few years, even the pursuit of it had often saved his sanity.

Flutters of calm touched him today and after several hours, he strolled home in the bright heat of early summer, feeling pleasantly energized.

On his porch, however, were the gory remains of a robin. The head, wings and tail were scattered beneath a chair, surrounded with a few loose gray feathers.

"Damned cat," Alexander swore, and found a shovel to remove the carcass. Piwacket, the murderer, slept serenely below a rosebush in the backyard. The mangy tom opened one eye as Alexander began to dig a shallow hole.

"The only thing that comforts me, Piwacket," he said to the animal, "is that soon you'll be much too fat to climb a tree." He frowned, eyeing the rippling, dusty belly that billowed before the cat like a sail. "It amazes me that you can move fast enough to catch even a robin."

Piwacket yawned and flopped back down into the warm dirt. Despite himself, Alexander grinned—few creatures were as unrepentantly degenerate as his cat.

He spent the afternoon gardening, taking pleasure in the feel of the warm sun on his bare head and arms, in the rich smell of the earth and the damp feel of it on his hands. He weeded between sprouting marigolds and his late wife's energetic lilies, and transplanted the tiny purple and blue violas that would create such lovely contrast to his collection of roses as the season progressed.

By dinnertime, he was satisfyingly sweaty and dirty, his arms and hands nicked from thorns and rocks. He showered, broiled a steak and sat down with a bottle of ale and the newspaper.

All according to schedule.

When he settled in the library for a nightcap of cognac and a little reading, that, too, was well within his routine. A breeze danced in through the French doors that led to his garden, carrying with it the relaxing scent of earth and wet grass.

He picked up a paperback suspense novel from the lamp table and read, sipping cognac in the quiet evening. Piwacket padded in on enormous paws and flopped his ragged, unkempt body at Alexander's feet. He meowed, but Alexander ignored him.

Annoyed, Piwacket jumped up to Alexander's desk, batting halfheartedly at pens and paperclips to watch them drop to the floor. Turning a page in his book with studious quiet, Alexander nonetheless smiled.

Next the scruffy animal leaped with surprising grace for his outrageous size to the lamp table. For a moment, he sat there, tail flicking, then reached out a paw and stuck it into the cognac, toppling the glass in the process. Alexander caught it before much was spilled, then shooed the tom off the table. "I thought we settled this," Alexander said with annoyance, dropping a paper napkin on the mess. "It's bad enough you don't purr, that you kill birds and leave me their heads, that you snore and knock things over, but you're also an alcoholic!"

Piwacket blinked, licking his whiskers. His yellow gaze was focused intently upon the cognac-soaked napkin. Alexander almost threw it into the dustbin near the desk, then thought better of it. He'd be picking up little scraps of paper in the morning, and Piwacket would have a bellyache from devouring the napkin.

"Come on," he told the animal his wife had rescued—against Piwacket's protests—from an alley behind a Denver hospital. "I'll get you some food." Not that Pi would eat it. A single bag of commercial food lasted several months and in spite of that, the animal was grossly overweight. He fed himself on birds and snakes and squirrels when he was lucky enough, but would be content with spiders, beetles and garbage pickings if times were lean.

But the evening sprinkle of food in Piwacket's plastic dish was also part of Alexander's meticulously ordered life. As he bent over the dish, smelling a fresh night wind blow through the open back door, he wondered how much longer he would cling to the web of routines. It seemed he'd been noticing them all day, since the lovely Esther had made her comment.

As he'd stood in the doorway of her sweet-smelling shop, with sunshine streaming in to dance in her hair, he'd found her perceptiveness amusing and interesting. After a day of observation, however, he wondered if he'd grown too entrenched—if his life had any meaning beyond his habits and schedule.

Until his wife's death four years before, he'd felt no need of regular timetables except those relating to his classes and that sort of thing. After Susan's death from leukemia, he'd found himself unexpectedly unable to cope with even the smallest chores without planning them in advance. All meaning had been stolen from his life, and into the void, he placed routines. They had lent at least an appearance of order to the endless days.

Looking out the door to the glittering, starry sky, he shook his head. Even Susan would protest this long recovery. She, perhaps, above all.

So instead of ascending the stairs for a shower as was his habit, he wandered into the living room and flipped on the television, clicking through channels until he found the late show. Once he'd enjoyed watching old movies. How long since he'd indulged the pleasure?

He poured a second cognac in further defiance of habit and settled in.

Unfortunately he tuned into a tragic romance made in the thirties. As he watched, trying to stick to his resolve to break his mindless routines, he thought of Esther and his instant, heady attraction to her. There was a sense of vibrant sensuality about her, a zest and verve that drew him like nothing else could have.

Susan, too, had possessed that quality. Even his mother, Juliette, had been an extraordinarily vibrant woman.

And both had died young.

For a moment, he was reminded of the dark, soul-devouring despair he had known after Susan's death.

Each moment of each day had been an ordeal to somehow overcome.

Vitality was no guarantee of protection against life's capriciousness, he thought, and turned off the television. Better empty routines than the bleak despair.

Sunday mornings when the boys were home were Esther's favorite. The store was closed and there was time for a big, leisurely breakfast.

This morning, Daniel sprawled on the living-room couch, watching cartoons. Jeremy played in the dining room, wearing Superman pajamas complete with cape and a foreign legion hat. In the kitchen, Esther listened to U2 on a cassette player and danced as she made French toast. Heaven, she thought, flipping the toast in time to the music.

The phone rang and Esther cheerfully answered it, tucking the phone between her shoulder and chin.

"Hi," said Abe. "Are you making waffles?"

"No. Sausage, orange juice and French toast. You want to come? I'll throw in some scrambled eggs and cheese just for you."

Abe groaned. "Thanks, but it sounds like a zoo over there. I'm not up to it this morning."

"It is," Esther replied, unoffended by the running joke. "What's up?"

"I just wanted to find out if you were going to teach the class."

After Alexander's departure a few days before, the shop had been swamped with customers and Abe had left with a single wave of his hand. "Yes," she said. "As you knew full well I would."

"Good."

"You aren't matchmaking by any chance, are you?"

"Esther, please." His voice was thick with disdain. "That's hardly my style."

"Mmm," she said skeptically. "Not officially." She turned the toast in the pan, satisfied at the golden finish. "But when I told you about the man in the dojo, you must have known who I was talking about."

"Yeah, I figured it was him. It didn't seem important."

Esther twisted her mouth, sure he was matchmaking now. "Sure, sure. What do you know about him?"

"Not much, really. He's been teaching me tai chi and we talk sometimes." Abe coughed uncomfortably. "He's a widower."

Her heart plummeted. There was the tragedy she had seen in his eyes. "Recent?"

"No. At least a few years."

Esther thought of his leonine grace and power at the dojo. "I'm intrigued," she admitted out of long habit. It was impossible for her to hide anything much from Abe.

"I thought you would be," he said and laughed. "Bye, Esther." He hung up without giving her a chance to say anything in return.

"Brat," she muttered, glaring at the phone. But as usual, Abe had accurately pegged her. Alexander Stone was the first man in ages to have caught her eye. There was something about him . . .

A wounded lion, she thought with a sigh. Damn Abe. He knew the last thing in the world she needed was another man with scars on his soul.

After breakfast, Daniel suggested a "city hike." They packed a lunch in a backpack and set off, walking the city blocks to view newly blooming flowers.

The neighborhood was one in which people took their exercise in the open air, against the backdrop of the Flatirons and the incredible blue of the Colorado sky. As they strolled, an older couple in neat sweat suits walked by, and a runner with earphones attached to his head dashed intently by them.

Daniel walked next to his mother, sometimes holding her hand. Jeremy played raven, running ahead of them with his arms outstretched as wings, cawing every so often. Several times, a real raven answered him.

Daniel watched. "Why is he so noisy, Mommy?"

"I don't know, honey. It drives you crazy, doesn't it?"

"Sometimes." He looked at her with enormous blue eyes. "But you know what I think?"

"What?"

"He's really going to be good at gym when he goes to school next year."

Esther grinned. "You're probably right."

"Maybe he can help me."

"Are you still having trouble?"

He shrugged. "I can't throw things very well or catch them, either. It seems like I figure it out, and then, it just doesn't work the way I want it to."

"Everybody is good at different things." She leaned toward him and in a confidential tone said, "I was terrible at gym."

Daniel brightened. "You were?"

"The worst."

He took her hand. "If you had a hundred people and only five of them were good at gym, that would be five percent."

She looked at him. "Have you been studying percentages?" First grade seemed a bit early for that.

"No," he said with a shrug. "I just read about them the other day."

"I'm impressed."

It would be impossible for a woman to have two more disparate children than she. Daniel was her little thinker, a child who'd memorized long books at two and added simple numbers by three. At four, he started reading and subtracting. And yet, it was never enough to satisfy him. Each new thing led him to something else. Already his room was littered with Encyclopedia Brown books and magazines about computer games and a huge text on simple science experiments. He was cautious, meticulous and prone to horrid rages of frustration.

Gifted his teachers said.

"Hey, Mommy," he said. "What's in the back of Rafael underwear?"

"What?"

"The sais." He burst out laughing.

Esther laughed, too—he was, after all, only six years old. "Where'd you get that?"

"I made it up. What's Donatello's favorite sport?"

"What?"

"Bo-ling."

"You're good at this. Are there more?"

"No, I haven't thought of anymore yet."

She nodded, and called to Jeremy, who had wandered a little too far ahead. When they got to the park, she settled on a blanket near the slides and swings. The children climbed over the playground while Esther read a book. After lunch, they headed back home, walking past the small shops and boutiques that lined the edges of the campus.

"Can we get an ice-cream cone?" Jeremy asked, pointing toward a man with a cart under an umbrella.

Just beyond was the dojo, and Esther realized with an embarrassed little shock that she'd deliberately led the children in this direction in hopes of seeing the attractive Alexander. And as if fate were punishing her for her cheekiness, who should emerge from said dojo but the man himself.

He caught sight of them and waved. To cover her embarrassment, Esther agreed to ice cream for the boys and paid for it, watching Alexander approach from the corner of her eye.

Daniel tugged her arm. "Mommy," he said urgently. "That's the man from karate. You should see him do stuff. He's better than *sensei.*"

"Is he?" Esther smiled. "I'm going to be working with him this summer. Maybe he'd show you some things if you asked."

A single look from those dark blue eyes expressed it all—wonder, delight, excitement, hope. Daniel glanced back toward Alexander and Esther watched something else replace the radiance—wariness.

She felt the same odd mix of emotions reflected within her own heart. Alexander's curls were tousled, falling rakishly over his broad forehead, and he walked toward them with the easy grace of an athletic, fit man. He wore jeans and a crisp, cream-colored shirt, unbuttoned at the neck and rolled casually below his elbows. The simple combination was elegant on his lean body, and Esther found herself eyeing the triangle of golden flesh visible at the edge of his shirt. A distinct quiver shook her. No man should look that good, *that* artlessly. It wasn't fair.

"Hello," he said, joining them.

Again Esther was struck with the richness of his deep voice. "Hi."

He ordered a cone for himself and paid for it. "Are you headed home or away?" he asked.

"Home. We've been to the park."

"I'll walk with you, then." He looked down at her and in his eyes, which were a very deep navy this afternoon, was a twinkle. "Unless you mind?"

Terrific, Esther thought. She'd been caught lasciviously eyeing his body once too often. "I don't mind."

Daniel tugged Esther's hand gently in reminder. "Alexander, I'd like to introduce my children. Boys, this is Mr. Stone." She gave him a quizzical glance. "Or is it Dr. Stone?"

"Actually, if you don't mind, I'd prefer Alexander."

"Okay. Boys, this is Alexander Stone. This is Daniel."

Daniel proffered a hand with the bearing and manners of a prep-school trainee. "Hello."

"It's a pleasure to meet you, Daniel," Alexander said, taking the boy's hand with the solemnity Daniel seemed to expect. Esther gave him a grateful smile.

Jeremy was cawing in a circle. "The raven there is Jeremy," Esther said, tongue in cheek.

Noticing the grown-ups' attention had shifted toward him, Jeremy giggled, dancing even more wildly.

"Jeremy," said Daniel, "is never, *ever* still or quiet."

"I see."

Introductions completed, Esther nibbled her ice cream and started walking. Alexander and the boys walked along with her, all of them attacking their cones. A group of summer tourists, sunburned and winded in the high altitude, passed. One woman smiled at Esther, and she realized they probably looked like a family. Again her thoughts embarrassed her and she cast around for something to say. "How long have you been studying martial arts?" she asked.

"A long, long time." He glanced at her. "I was one of those skinny children who need all the help they can get. My mother thought it would be good for me to learn."

"It must have done the trick," Esther commented. "I find it hard to imagine you as a ninety-eight-pound weakling."

"Thank you." He gave her a devilish smile, then caught a dollop of chocolate ice cream just before it fell.

Esther glanced away, but couldn't entirely shut out the sense of his lean, taut body walking alongside hers. "Which discipline do you practice?"

"Several, actually. Mr. Kobayashi is tutoring me in *shokotan* at the moment, while I'm sharing my knowledge of tai chi and *hsing-i*."

"Isn't that sort of unusual, to practice more than one discipline?"

"No, not really. We all choose a particular form that suits us, I think. But there are things to be learned from others." He looked at Daniel. "How long have you been studying with *sensei?*"

Shyly, Daniel shrugged. "Not very long." He raised his enormous robin's-egg eyes to the man beside him.

"It takes a long time to be as good as you are, doesn't it?"

"Well, what you've seen me doing is not the same as what you do with Mr. Kobayashi. It's easier, I think." He touched his shoulder. "Would you like me to teach you a few things the next time you're there?"

A blaze of brightness flared in Daniel's eyes for an instant, and then his lids swept down and he licked his cone. "If you want."

Jeremy grabbed Esther's hand, nearly tugging it out of the socket in his exuberance. "I want to!" he cried.

"Take it easy, honey." She gave Alexander a smile, raising her eyebrows.

"'Never, ever still or quiet,'" Alexander said and amusement lightened the planes of his face. Esther found herself noticing his mouth for the first time. It was mobile and sensual, his lips firm and full. She didn't know how she'd missed that before. Ice cream dripped on her thumb, and glad of the distraction, she licked it away.

Their walk had carried them into a residential neighborhood of older clapboard homes. The sidewalks were made up of tiny cement squares. Old-fashioned lilac bushes, feathery white spirea and enormous stands of purple, yellow and white irises filled the grassy yards. Alexander paused before one freshly painted Victorian. "This is my stop," he said.

"This is yours?" Esther asked with delight. "I've always loved this place." It had a wide wooden porch that circled around the side, and windows in odd nooks and crannies. She grinned. "You know what I've always noticed about it?"

He smiled, inclining his big lion head. "Tell me."

Esther pointed to the second story, at a window open to the breeze. Set before it was a heavy ceramic pitcher and basin for washing. "That's the most serene window I've ever seen."

A network of lines creased the skin below his eyes as he smiled. He looked first at Esther and then at the window. "I've never noticed before." He chuckled. "Luckily you've never seen the inside—your picture would be quite transformed."

"Why?"

"It's a junk room, I'm afraid." Comfortably, he gestured toward the house. "Can I persuade you to come in for a glass of tea or something?"

She wasn't really quite ready to leave behind his easy company. "All right. Thank you." Then she looked at Jeremy and back at the neatly painted house. "Please tell me you don't have rooms full of priceless antiques."

To her surprise, Alexander laughed. "It's just a house, Esther. He won't injure anything."

Again, she found herself smiling at him in gratitude, and for an instant she was caught in the gentle admiration she saw on his face. Shyly she turned to call for Jeremy as Daniel followed Alexander up the steps.

Inside, she was relieved to find that his statement was true. There were no spindly chairs or brocaded sofas. The rooms were large and scattered with comfortable groupings of chairs, ottomans and tables. Braided rugs covered the floors.

"You see?" Alexander said, gesturing broadly. "Nothing to worry about."

She nodded and her attention was caught by a series of framed prints on the long west wall. "Oh," she sighed, going forward to examine them. "Maxfield Parrish. They're beautiful!"

On a second wall were scenes from the King Arthur legend, done in the same Victorian mode. "Look, Daniel," she said. "Guinevere, King Arthur and Lancelot. And Camelot."

Behind her Alexander said, "That was my favorite legend as a child."

She turned. "Mine, too. But I never believed it was a legend. I think it really happened—maybe not exactly the way they say it did, but there was a Camelot and a great king."

"And a beautiful queen?" He lifted an eyebrow.

"Yes."

He shook his head. "Perhaps you need my class as much as any of the students. History is never as romantic as we'd like it to be."

"Perhaps," she said lightly, "you're in need of a pair of rose-colored glasses."

He met her gaze for a minute, and a thousand things rushed over the surface of his eyes. "I don't think so," he said finally.

A fat gray cat wandered into the room and leaped with surprising nimbleness into a chair, then stared at the lot of them with unmistakable malevolence in its yellow eyes. "Are we invading your territory?" Esther asked it quietly.

It was a scruffy Persian mix with missing tufts of fur and a fat face and enormous paws. One ear was battered, half torn away a long time ago. It glared at her.

"That's Piwacket," Alexander said. "Don't bother to treat him like a cat. He thinks he's a reincarnated pirate."

Esther considered the notion. "All he lacks is the eye patch."

Piwacket looked at Alexander with an almost human expression of smugness. As if he'd spoken, Alexander said, "Don't let it go to your head." He turned to the boys. "Would you like some tea, gentlemen?"

"No, thanks," Daniel said, speaking for both of them as he often did. "Can we play outside?"

"I don't mind."

"Go ahead," Esther said with a nod. As they raced for the door, she called, "Don't pick the flowers!"

That left Esther and Alexander standing in the middle of the room. She found her eyes traveling over the slice of skin visible at the unbuttoned edges of his shirt, and hurriedly dipped her head, brushing hair nervously from her face.

Alexander cleared his throat. "Well," he said. "Shall we go to the kitchen? I'll pour you a glass of tea."

It was crazy to have agreed to coming in, Esther thought. This man was way out of her league—he ought to be offering cool drinks to a lawyer or a sleekly intelligent psychologist, not a disheveled and motherly shopkeeper.

But since she'd already agreed, she followed him toward the back of the house, unwilling to be rude. She'd drink her tea and get away as quickly as she could.

Alexander led her into his kitchen, a spacious room with an oak table and long windows. He gestured Esther into a chair, then took tall glasses from a cupboard. "What did you think of the notes I sent you?"

"It looks like a great class," she said. "I think I'll be able to work out some lessons you'll like." She leaned on the table as he sat down across from her. "If I bring my plans to the first class, will that work all right?"

As he settled in his chair, Alexander was struck with her full beauty, just inches away from him. Her hair floated around her oval face in soft red waves, and her lips were as plump as September plums. The dress she wore this afternoon was as unusual as the other things he'd seen her in. It was a style copied from the thirties—a sheer black and floral pattern over a dark slip. Winking white rhinestone buttons traveled up the front.

Alexander had been finding it difficult since he'd first caught sight of her in the street to avoid the alluring glimpses of pale flesh he could see beneath the sheer fabric. Sitting so close to her, he found it impossible. Beneath the loose-fitting sheer, her round shoulders and arms were delectably female, and the dark slip beneath caressed her breasts in a way that conjured up distinctly erotic visions.

And yet, there was no way the dress could be thought of as anything but feminine and lovely.

"Alexander? Will that be all right?"

He looked at her. To hell with routines—a man would be insane to resist a goddess fallen into his midst. "Why don't you have dinner with me on Friday, and bring it to me then?"

A slow smile bloomed on her lips, and a sleepily pleased look flared in her dark eyes. It was an echo of the demure sexuality of her dress. "I'd like that," she said.

"Good," he said firmly and forced himself to straighten, shake off the heat in his loins and act like the gentleman he'd been raised to be. "I'll be by to pick you up at seven."

Chapter Three

The next week whirled by in the blur that seemed to mark early summer for Esther. Daniel passed with stellar grades from first grade to second and happily put aside scholarly pursuits for the heartier pleasures of bike riding and baiting his little brother. She planted her vegetable garden with tomatoes, peppers, garlic and onions, along with basil, sage and bay leaves, all for the spaghetti sauce she made each year to sell in the shop. It was amazing what people would pay for one jar of "one hundred percent organically grown homemade pasta and spaghetti sauce."

She took her children on picnics and swimming, and set aside a plot for each of them to grow what they chose. Daniel planted enormous sunflowers, filling his whole space with them. Jeremy chose watermelon and popcorn.

In between the other activities, she found herself daydreaming about the elusive Alexander. All week she was alternately delighted and sick about the idea of going out to dinner with him. It was the first date she'd had in a long, long time, for one thing. Her divorce had left her wary of men, particularly when it seemed most of them were interested primarily in a tumble in the hay.

And what did she really know about Alexander? Aside from the fact that he had a riveting, lean body and changeable, intriguing eyes, of course. That sort of physical attraction could be put down to hormones—not a very reliable barometer of a man's possibilities as far as she was concerned.

But it had been a long time since she'd even felt a quickening in a man's presence. She'd forgotten how delicious it was to imagine kisses. Particularly when the mouth she imagined kissing was sensual and firm and surrounded with a silky-looking beard and mustache.

As she stood on her dining-room table Friday afternoon to replace a burned-out light bulb, her thoughts were still chasing themselves in circles, and she blew out an aggravated breath. Facts.

Only one should matter to her: the fact that he was a man who had experienced enough tragedy that it had turned his beard prematurely silver. That alone ought to set the warning bells ringing in her mind.

"Mommy!" called Daniel, slamming through the front door. "Daddy's here."

"Tell him to come in!" she yelled in return.

"I can hear you!" John yelled from beside the table, imitating her bellow.

She laughed. "Sorry. I'll be done in a minute."

John crossed his arms. "You must spend a fortune on light bulbs. Every time I come over, you're changing that one."

"Hardly." She replaced the glass covering and jumped down from the table, and as she did, she remembered that she had been changing this very bulb the last time he had come to get the kids. "We spend a lot of time in here," she said, more to herself than to John.

"It's the only room with heat, right?" he said, tongue-in-cheek.

Esther rolled her eyes, declining to respond to the barb. "I'll call Jeremy. They've already got their things together."

He picked up the used light bulb and followed her into the kitchen. Just then, Jeremy bounded in. "Daddy!"

John hugged him hard, kissing the rosy cheek. Esther admired the picture they made, her dark little son and his tall, reed-thin father.

But as she looked at her former husband, she realized she didn't think he was handsome anymore. Once he'd looked like the devil himself in her eyes. Now he looked like the rake that he was, and it amazed her that she hadn't seen it then.

He playfully spanked Jeremy and put him down. "You ready to go fishing, little buddy?"

"Fishing?" Esther repeated with narrowed eyes. "Where are you going to go fishing?"

He gave her a look of impatience. "Just in the creek, Esther. I'm not takin' them on a boat or anything like that. Are you ever going to learn to trust me with these kids?"

"Maybe when you're a hundred." Then she smiled in apology. For all his failings as a faithful husband, he was a thoughtful, careful father. It was one of the things that had kept her hanging on as long as she had. "So I worry," she said, waving her hands. "What mother doesn't?"

John grinned back. "No good mom." He looked at Jeremy. "You go get your stuff and put it into the car." When the boy had raced off to do his bidding, John looked at Esther more seriously. "Have you given any more thought to letting me take them to the ranch?"

Esther took a deep breath. "I don't know. It's such a long trip."

"My dad is dying, Esther. He isn't gonna be around next summer."

"But won't two little boys be too much noise and bustle for an emphysema patient?" She caught his skeptical gaze. "Okay, I know. Not on a ranch. Are you going to teach them to ride horses?"

"I thought about it." He lifted his eyebrows and wryly asked, "You want me to get some helmets?"

Esther laughed. "Okay, I give. If they want to go, I guess I don't have any objections."

"Thanks, babe." He hugged her quickly. "I'll talk to them about it."

Their departure, amid hugs and kisses and forgotten stuffed animals, left the house quiet and empty. Esther wandered around, picking up. It was too bad, she thought as she carried a load of toys upstairs, that she and John had been unable to work things out. She had liked being married, having a family and people to take care of. It had been wonderful when John would come home and they all sat down to supper together, talking about the day.

And it was hard to be a single parent. She hated sending the boys off every other weekend. The rules at Daddy's house weren't quite the same as at Mommy's.

Hearing the self-pitying tone of her thoughts, she shook her head. What she had now was a hundred times better than what she'd had with John and she knew it.

Dumping the toys into the children's closet, she went to her own bedroom. A breeze lifted the lace curtains lightly, cool and sweet. As Esther settled by the window, she admired her flowers and the rich green of her lawn. None of it had been there when they had reclaimed the house four years ago. Her grandmother had spent the last years of her life in a nursing home, a period in which the house had been lackadaisically rented out to a series of tenants. Esther had been living in Denver and the problems with her marriage had necessarily drawn her attention away from anything outside herself. No one else had cared much about the lawns around the old house, and the management company hired by her grandmother had been remiss in repairs. As a result, there had been no yard left and the already deteriorating house had fallen into even deeper disrepair.

She smiled. Now the naked ladies and irises her grandmother had loved were springing up in the backyard. Pin-cushion flowers and larkspur lined the front walk. Even the house itself was coming along. Last winter, she had torn up the aging carpets in the front two rooms that comprised her shop and buffed the hardwood floors below. Door by door, threshold by threshold, she was redoing the woodwork.

One day her house would be as beautiful as the one Alexander lived in. It was worth it.

Alexander. Her stomach flipped again and she glanced at the clock. Two hours. What in the world was she going to wear?

Long buttery fingers of sunlight slanted through the trees as Alexander approached Esther's house. It was a beautiful evening, he thought, whistling as he rang the bell.

She flung open the door. In the instant it took for her to smile and push the screen aside for him to enter, he was nearly stunned by her beauty. Her hair had been tamed a bit with combs, but tendrils escaped to cling to her long white neck. Her cheeks glistened with a rosy glow and she'd put some shiny color on her mouth.

But it was the wide swath of her bare shoulders that seized him. All he could see for a moment was the pale expanse of naked flesh, as flawless as bridal satin above the simple green dress.

"Will this be all right?" she asked uncertainly. "I wasn't quite sure where we were going, so I wore something kind of in-between."

"It's beautiful," he said. "I'll be the envy of every man we see."

Her ripe grin flashed and she raised one eyebrow archly. "As I will be the envy of the women."

Both of them said nothing more for a moment, then as if aware of the absurdity of the moment, both laughed. "I'm a little out of practice with these things," she admitted.

"So am I," he said and took her hand. "If you'll forgive my mistakes, I'll overlook yours—not that I think you'll make any."

"Agreed."

Outside, he took her arm as they headed for his car. Esther paused on the sidewalk. "Are we going far?"

"Not at all. Would you like to walk?"

"It's such a beautiful evening."

He glanced at her feet, expecting high heels. Instead she wore simple black flats. She followed his gaze. "I'm tall enough without them," she explained. "I really hate heels."

There was a note of apology in her words. "I've never understood how women could stand them. And now we can enjoy ourselves without my having to be concerned over your feet."

She smiled and tucked her hand under his elbow.

As he had promised, the restaurant wasn't far. It was a small place, quiet, with a wide variety of foods on the menu. "I wasn't sure," Alexander said as they waited for the hostess, "if you were an organic sort of eater or not."

She laughed and leaned closer to him. In a confidential tone, she said, "I'm afraid I'm an infidel. I've got a fatal weakness for any food deemed evil by the Surgeon General."

The hostess led them to a small table in an intimate alcove. A fat candle burned in a jar next to the long windows that looked out toward campus. The sidewalks, while hardly as teeming as they would be later in the year, were filled with young people out for the evening.

Alexander ordered a Gibson and looked at Esther. "I'm not sure yet," she told the waitress, then bit her lip to hold back a wicked grin. "No, I know. Bring me a Gibson, too. On the rocks, with extra onions." With raised eyebrows, she looked at him. "May as well live dangerously."

"Not many young women in America drink Gibsons."

"I've never had one," she said. "But I used to make them for my father and they smelled wonderful."

Alexander grinned. "My wife despised the smell of them," he commented, then wondered if it was the wrong thing to say. It had come out without much thought.

Esther cocked her head. "Abe told me you're a widower. I'm sorry."

The direct confrontation of a subject most people avoided took Alexander by surprise. "Thank you."

"I'm divorced," she offered, taking a sip of water. "But I still sometimes feel married. Does that ever happen to you?"

Ordinarily he avoided this subject at all costs, but there was something so calm about Esther's attitude, he found himself not only unoffended but almost relieved. "Yes," he said. "We were married twelve years and however unfashionable it may sound, I was married at heart."

"It's not at all unfashionable in my book." She smiled broadly. "Especially since I had the sort of husband that never did understand what marriage was all about."

"I'm sorry," he said.

"Thank you." She bent her head to the menu and Alexander let his eyes linger on the gentle curve of her cheek and the slope of her creamy shoulder for a moment. Her husband must have been a fool.

* * *

When the waitress had delivered their drinks and taken their orders, Esther lifted her Gibson and tasted it experimentally. It was strong, but she had expected that of gin and pickled onions. It was also very good, as refreshing as it smelled.

"Well?" Alexander asked curiously.

"Not bad." She smiled at him, aware of a delightful sense of excitement and wonder at being here, alone with him. In the candlelight, his neat beard glittered with mahogany and silver lights and his eyes were so dark as to be nearly black. For the first time, she noticed his tie. The pattern, hand painted on silk, had seemed very ordinary at first. Now she realized it was made of whimsical, tiny cat faces. She grinned at him. "Clever," she said.

"Ah," he breathed, touching the tie with long brown fingers. His eyes twinkled. "I thought you might like it. It was a toss-up between this and one with swords."

So he wasn't as serious as he first appeared, she thought, delighted. "Where, speaking of cats, did you find that animal of yours?"

"Piwacket?" He gave her a wry twist of his lips. "My wife dragged him home from the hospital one night."

"That's an attack cat if I ever saw one."

"He's not so bad when you get to know him. He has even been known to purr once or twice."

"You don't strike me as the sort of man who would like cats."

"Oh?" His mouth curved in humor. "What sort of pet ought I have, then?"

Esther pursed her lips in consideration. She ran through the possibilities in her mind—a terrier? Too nervous. Labradors? Too dependent. Birds? Too fussy. A picture of him with a tiger flashed through her mind—two fierce creatures, sleek and strong, with a veneer of civilization masking the wildness below.

Her blood quickened at the picture, and she wondered what it would be like to unleash the passion she saw in his lightning eyes and sensual mouth, heard in his dusky voice.

Aloud she said, "I take it back. A rough old Persian cat suits you just right, although an obnoxious Siamese might even be better."

"My mother loved Siamese cats. We had bundles of them—or at least what she said were Siamese. She insisted most black cats were, and some pure white."

"Does she still live in England?"

He glanced toward the darkened window. "She died when I was sixteen."

"Fate hasn't been kind to you, has she?" Esther said, pierced at the thought of leaving her own children before they were fully grown. And then she could have bitten her tongue, because there was a swift and fleeting bleakness on his face for an instant. "Alexander, I'm sorry. I don't know what made me say that."

He recovered so quickly that she wondered if the bleakness had been a product of her imagination. "It's all right," he said.

"What was she like, your mother?"

He settled back in his chair and gazed outside for a moment. Then he looked back at Esther. "Juliette was—" he paused, his mobile mouth shifting "—eccentric." He raised a laconic eyebrow. "She was a spiritualist—believed in ghosts and mediums and all kinds of odd things."

Esther laughed. She had been expecting the story of a hardworking housewife. "Go on."

"She ran a little occult bookstore and gave Tarot readings and that sort of thing in the back. A New Ager, you'd call her now."

"Was she good? Or did she just tell fortunes to make people feel better?"

He lifted his chin, touching his beard in what Esther assumed must be an habitual gesture. "I don't know. She lost her whole family in the Blitz and I've always thought it sent her a bit over the edge."

"Really?" Esther leaned forward, intrigued. "What about your father?"

"They were divorced when I was very small. I didn't see much of him."

Again Esther felt that strange prick of sorrow on behalf of the boy he once had been. With it came a need to hug him close to her, the way she might hug one of her sons.

Catching the drift of her thoughts, she straightened abruptly. Would she never learn? Men who needed healing were her specialty—and once they were healed, they went along on their merry way. She would not even *consider* trying to heal the wounds of this man.

The waitress appeared with their food and Esther was grateful for the distraction. She had ordered a huge pork burrito, smothered with green chili and cheese. Lifting an eyebrow toward Alexander, she said, "See? Enough cholesterol to strangle a horse!"

"Do horses need to watch their cholesterol?" he asked dryly.

She laughed, relieved the conversation had taken a lighter turn. And as they ate, it stayed in the polite range. They discussed food, which Esther wryly admitted with a gesture to her rounded figure, was one of her favorite topics. He had predictably English tastes in food and a rather precise list of dislikes that amused her: fresh spinach, brussels sprouts, okra. She told him of her children's preferences in food, which narrowed down to one fact: if Daniel loved it, Jeremy hated it and vice versa.

After dinner, he suggested a walk in the mild evening. For an instant, she hesitated.

He reached over to take her hand. "I'm not sure where it happened, Esther, but I lost you somewhere."

Esther swallowed and looked away, unable as always to hide her thoughts.

His voice, when he spoke again, was teasing. "Whatever it was, I hope you'll at least grant me the pleasure of a walk this evening."

His long, callused fingers stroked the back of her hand, more persuasive than he knew. A shimmering, liquid silver passed from his hand into hers and danced all the way down her spine, then doubled and traveled back the way it had come. He couldn't be unaware of it.

As she met his eyes, she watched the irises change from the near black the candlelight gave them to a lighter, almost greenish hue. Now he didn't look at all like a man in need of healing, but one who would deliver it instead.

She took a breath against the longing she felt for that soothing touch on her own soul. She ought to thank him for dinner and go home, but found she couldn't resist the temptation to spend just a little more time with him tonight.

She turned her hand to meet his palm to palm, taking pleasure in the shock of awareness the callused heart of his palm gave her. "It's much too beautiful an evening to waste," she said.

Outside in the night, with the sounds of unfettered collegiate excitement ringing in the air, Alexander took her hand. As they crossed the street to walk under the canopy of trees on campus, he asked, "Where are your children tonight?"

"They spend every other weekend with their father."

"Hmm," he murmured noncommittally. "Do you mind?"

"Sometimes. I miss them on Sunday mornings when they aren't here. We have big breakfasts—" She broke off, sure she had already spent more time than she should have talking about her children.

"And?"

She looked up at him. The streetlights gave his curly dark hair a halo of misty light. "You must get tired of my continual chatter about my children."

"No." He looked toward the thicket of trees ahead with a pensive expression. "I always wanted some of my own. Your two are the sort I always imagined. They're beautiful, you know."

"Of course I know," she said, laughing. "They're mine!"

"I mean it. They're very handsome boys. Do they look like your husband?"

Again Esther laughed. "Does that mean they couldn't possibly look like me because they're handsome?"

"Ah," he said regretfully, leaning a hair closer to her. "You promised to overlook my little gaffes."

"You're right. I did." Tossing her head, she said, "The boys look very much like their father."

"Have you been divorced long?"

It seemed a personal question, but she understood his asking it. "Three years. My house was the final straw."

"Your house?"

"John absolutely refused to sink a penny into it— said it was a white elephant, or someone else in the family would have taken it."

"But you love it."

Esther glanced at him, surprised again at his perceptiveness. "Yes, I really do. My great-grandfather built it for his wife and it's been in the family all those years. It would have broken my heart to let it go."

"There's value in old things," he replied. "I think you Yanks are only just now learning that."

Esther grinned. "But, Professor, doesn't valuing old things lead to romanticizing them?"

"No," he said firmly. "We can certainly admire them, but it is very important to avoid attaching magic and wonder to them."

"Why?"

"Well, a sword is a good example. It's a beautiful bit of craftsmanship and it feels wonderful in your hand, but it was made to kill people."

"That's oversimplification, Professor Stone," she argued. "Those swords were also protection." She paused, looking toward the points of pine trees against the starry sky. Something about his insistence upon harsh reality disturbed her. "And how can you take a legend like the one about King Arthur and reduce it to facts and figures?''

''You don't.''

''But you said—''

He smiled down at her. ''I merely said I didn't believe it.''

They paused on a bridge spanning a small pond. Light spilled over the water, wavering in broken patterns in the blackness. ''Then why do you have the prints on your walls?''

''To remind me of my shed romantic illusions.'' He braced one hip against the stone railing.

''So, once you *did* believe,'' she said.

He leaned on the stone railing. As he seemed to mull over his reply, she watched his thoughts play over his craggy face. The reflected light from the water caught the silver in his hair and beard and threw shadows over his generous, mobile mouth. Rubbing her fingers unconsciously against her thumb, she wondered how those curls and beard would feel. When he looked at her again, she had forgotten what their conversation had been.

''Once,'' he said quietly, ''I did believe.'' He reached out and touched her cheek with the backs of his fingers. ''Looking at you now, I am inclined to believe in Guinevere again.''

Esther lowered her eyes, feeling strangely shy and electrically aroused all at once. She was afraid her eyes would show how lusty his fingers on her face made her feel—and where would it lead?

He stepped forward until his long, lean body was only inches from her own. In silence, he let his fingers travel over her jaw and down her neck. She looked up and found his eyes watching his hand as his fingertips grazed the flesh of her bared shoulder.

He smelled like soap and spicy cologne and gin. The scent mixed with the perfume of pines carried by a breeze. Her nerves were so taut that when the breeze floated over her neck, she nearly shuddered. How long? she thought. How long since a man had made her feel this way? How long since she'd kissed anyone, or felt the hard muscles and angles of a man's body against her own?

Too long, she thought as he curled his fingers around her neck and lifted her chin with his other hand. Their chests touched lightly, and their thighs. And then their mouths.

His lips were full against her own, and asked nothing at first. The hairs of his mustache and beard added a richness of sensation that she hadn't expected, and she raised her palm to touch the masculine adornment, finding it as silky as she had imagined. His jaw was strong below the fur.

After a moment, he tugged her closer and Esther found his lips also fulfilled the sensual promise they held. He kissed her slowly, as if each millimeter of her mouth warranted lingering exploration. He brushed kisses over the bow of her upper lip, the swell of the lower, the corners on either side. All without hurry.

Esther felt her spine slowly weaken, the tiny bones refusing to support her. And she melted into him, languorously aware of how hard his chest and arms were. Kissing was never given the attention it deserved, she thought vaguely. How exhilarating to find someone who agreed it was a delight unto itself.

And in that spirit, she let herself go a little. She explored the dips and curves of his lips, let his beard caress her chin, his mustache her upper lip and nose. His long fingers laced through her hair, cupping her scalp firmly.

She couldn't have said how long they stood there above the pond in the darkness, just kissing. Her heart dropped into a slow thudding pattern and she couldn't tell if a minute or century had passed, only that she'd somehow fallen adrift in his arms.

When he lifted his head, his eyes showed the same glaze of wonder Esther felt. He simply looked into her face for a long moment. "Perhaps," he said in a roughened, low voice, "you will lead me back to the legends, instead of the other way around."

Then he took her hand and they walked on in the mild night. Esther risked a glance at him once and found he had a bemused expression on his face that seemed to mirror her own feelings. She smiled to herself and continued to walk silently next to him.

After a time, they started speaking again, about the class and the things they would be doing. They parted on the porch. He didn't kiss her good-night, and Esther didn't expect it.

Inside, she leaned against the door and let the bottled-up emotions of the evening flow from her. Healing, she thought. There was a matter of healing she needed to remember. She was the fix-it lady—whatever a man's ills, Esther had a need to try to soothe them.

And if ever a man needed the healing of a loving woman, Alexander did. The trouble was, his wounds were as serious in their way as the shrapnel that riddled Abe's physical body. To find true healing, the shards of the past would have to be removed.

Sobering, she walked upstairs, thinking of her ex-husband. John of the vague father and alcoholic mother; John who had left home at twelve and had tattoos on his arms before he was sixteen. She had never managed to teach him how to love a woman and no one ever would—his scars were too deep. Over the years, he'd made peace with his father, and he loved his sons the way he had once longed to be loved, but no woman would ever overcome the betrayal of his mother.

As she shed her clothes in preparation for a bath, she could see now that her primary attraction to her former husband had been the need to heal him the way she'd healed stray cats with her herbal lore as a teenager. Trouble was, not all healing took. And she'd wasted almost ten years on him.

Wasted? No. She had her children. And a boy, properly raised, didn't need healing as a man.

That was her task, she decided, raising her two boys into adults healthy enough to withstand the blows of life. She couldn't allow any man to interfere with that.

But as she slipped into the warm, lavender-scented water of her bath, she felt again the heavy thudding of her heart that Alexander's kiss had aroused. She knew herself well enough to know that if he decided to pursue her, she'd be hard put to resist.

Chapter Four

Saturdays were always busy at the shop and the day after Esther's date with Alexander was no different, a fact for which she gave silent thanks. It kept her mind from lingering too much upon the lion man, he of the changeable eyes and beautiful lips and lingering sorrows.

Abe appeared late in the afternoon. Esther kneeled in front of the long shelves, straightening a row of natural cosmetics: shampoos made with herbs and exotic plant oils, clay facial masks, oatmeal soap and baking powder deodorant. When the bell rang, she looked up. "Greetings, stranger," she said to Abe, getting to her feet. "Where have you been all week?"

He shrugged in resignation. "Had a bad couple of days—I had to hang around the house mainly."

"Oh, Abe, I'm sorry." She hugged him, feeling the stiffness in his body. "Have a seat and let me fix you some tea."

"I'm all right today," he protested. "I had a walk around campus and worked out the kinks." In contrast to his words, however, he sank with studied effort into the rattan love seat, grunting a little as he settled. "Any evil doughnuts stashed away in the kitchen?"

Esther grinned. "Sorry—I only allowed myself to buy two sticky buns this morning, since I'm by myself."

Abe groaned at the missed treat. "With nuts?"

"Guilty." She glanced at her watch. "If you can hang around for an hour, I'll make something dreadfully wicked for us to share after I close."

"How wicked?"

In mock fear, she glanced over her shoulder at the empty shop, then whispered, "Chocolate fondue."

"Pretty bad. I guess I'm going to have to stay and help you eat it."

"Will you get some strawberries from the market? Or would you rather rest?"

"Hell, no, I don't want to rest." Using his cane to lever himself into a standing position, he added, "I'm sick of resting."

"You can at least have a cup of tea before you run off."

He shook his head, eyes glittering. A long lock of dark hair fell on his forehead and he tossed it back defiantly. "For chocolate fondue, I can do anything."

Esther laughed and returned to her straightening as he left. When the stock was again neatly presented, she turned back the pages of a small notebook that she kept by the cash register. Three pages were filled with precise accounts of every sale she had made today. From the list she would do inventory and ordering, and as backup, she handwrote receipts for each purchase.

It was a laborious process and friends constantly extolled the ease a computer would give her. Bent over the lists this afternoon, wearily noting boxes of henna sold—one natural, one chestnut—jars of jam—two each of crab apple and rosehip—and bottles of juice from the refrigerated unit that had been one of her heftiest and most valuable investments for the store, she realized once again that it would be fabulous to have a computer. Unfortunately it was completely out of her budget at the moment. Perhaps by fall she would be able to look at used systems.

Footsteps on the front porch alerted her to the presence of a customer and with a sigh, Esther looked at her watch again. In spite of her wish that she could just be done with the long day, she plastered a welcoming smile on her face and looked up.

It was Alexander, his face suffused with healthy color. He brought with him the smell of the outdoors, a mixture of sunshine and earth and a good wind. For a moment, she forgot her resolve to keep him at arm's length. "Hello," she said warmly. "You must have spent the day outside."

He grinned, pausing just inside the door. "How did you know?"

"Your nose is sunburned." She smiled, surprised in a secret part of herself at how fiercely pleased she was to see him again. In contrast to the mild sunburn, his eyes were nearly neon blue and his unruly dark curls with their tiny silver accents tumbled in disarray over his head. He wore khaki chinos with a cream-colored polo shirt. In combination with the healthy color in his face, the clothes gave him an effortlessly elegant look. Self-consciously, she smoothed her dress and touched her hair, wondering how her own apparel had fared through the day. "What brings you here this afternoon?" she asked a little breathlessly.

"I was out for a walk," he said with a shrug. "Thought I'd stop in and say hello."

"I'm glad you did," she said, and realized that if she were planning to keep him at arm's length, that was probably the wrong thing to say. But rather than retract it, she rounded the counter that separated them. "Can I offer you something?"

A quirk of humor lifted one corner of his mouth. "Careful," he teased in his rich voice, "I may ask for more than you will give."

The earthy nature of the light comment was unmistakable and Esther felt hot. She lowered her eyes. "How about a sample of Esther's Special Herb Tea?" she asked, bustling toward a coffeemaker in the corner where she brewed the tea. "I know how you English love your hearty blends, but this is very special and very nice and I think you might enjoy it." As she spoke, she busied her hands with a mug. Pouring the clear red-brown liquid, she inhaled the citrusy scent of hibiscus.

"I make it myself," she continued, vaguely aware that she was babbling. "It took a few years to figure out the best recipe. I think I've finally got it right, but who knows?" She shrugged. "I may change it again."

Alexander accepted the heavy mug of tea. On his craggy face was an expression of amusement. Esther flushed for the second time in three minutes, mentally calling herself a ninny.

Ceremoniously he lifted the cup to his lips, his eyes fastened on her face. He cocked an eyebrow. "You're right. It isn't English tea at all, but it's delicious nonetheless."

"I'm all out of lemonade," she said and then touched her lips, wishing she could call back the words. Rather irrelevant, after all.

"This is fine." He gestured toward the chair. "May I?"

"Of course. Enjoy it. I have to finish a few notes and then I'll join you."

Safely behind the counter, Esther bent her head over the lists, hoping the simple business task would calm her. It did not. Like a ten-year-old with a crush, she couldn't concentrate while he was in the room. It was hard to breathe. Biting her lip, she glanced up at him through her lashes.

He was studying her with a curiously sober expression. Esther straightened and frowned. "Is something wrong?"

"No." His expression didn't lighten. "I was about to ask you the same thing."

"Not at all." She twisted the pencil in her fingers, then lifted a shoulder helplessly. "You just flustered me a little, that's all."

"Did I now?" he smiled and stepped forward. "I'm honored." He stretched a hand over the counter and lightly touched her cheek. "Then perhaps I can persuade you to come out with me again tonight. A simple meal?"

A long ray of sunlight arched through the window and splashed into his beard. Esther admired the silver and dark brown threads, remembering how silky that hair had felt against her chin. She warred with herself for a moment, trying to remember the resolve she had made to concentrate on her children, rather than a man who needed emotional mending.

The trouble was, he didn't look at all like a man in need of healing. He looked strong and controlled, his eyes glimmering with sparks of desire as they flickered over her face, her lips, her hair. A fleeting but acute vision swept her mind, a vision of his civilized veneer undone by passion—

She swallowed. Perhaps her mind had also manufactured the picture of him as a man in need of healing. "I'd love to," she said in reply to his dinner invitation—then remembered Abe. "But I can't. I've just sent Abe to get strawberries for a fondue."

"All right," he said. "Perhaps another day."

"Or maybe you'd like to join us?" Esther returned hopefully. "It's not an ordinary sort of meal, though." She cleared her throat a little ruefully. "Actually we'll just be having dessert."

Just then, Abe appeared with an overflowing net bag. Ripe red strawberries peeked through the top. She could also see a bakery angel food cake, pears and apples, and a chunk of white cheese.

"If we can't make ourselves sick on this, we're too greedy to live," Abe commented, plopping the bag on the counter. He grinned at Alexander. "Contrary to current opinion, Esther believes the way to health is gluttony."

Esther slapped his arm. "I do not!" Lifting her chin in an effort to assemble some dignity, she tugged the cake out of the mesh. "But a little greed can be good for the soul." She glanced at Alexander. "Will you stay?"

"I don't want to impose."

"She's a big eater, Alexander," Abe said, "but I'll make sure she doesn't get it all."

Esther glared at him, then looked at Alexander, who had a suspiciously amused expression in his eyes. "I do have a few normal things to eat, too," she said. "I'll make us all some ham sandwiches first, then we can open a bottle of wine in the backyard and eat the fondue out there as the sun sets."

Alexander gave her a lazy grin, one eyebrow cocking in consideration. There was something so sensually promising in the expression that Esther swallowed. A second detailed vision of him completely tousled and wild with leonine passion assaulted her.

She lowered her eyes, shocked at herself.

"It would be my pleasure to share such a feast," he said in his rumbling voice, "but only if you will allow me to add a contribution of my own."

"Of course!" She glanced at her watch. "I'll put Abe to work making sandwiches while I wash up. A half hour?"

Again a promise danced in his eyes. "A half hour it is." Whistling, he exited.

Abe swung around, leaning his elbows on the counter. "Are you going to seduce him with strawberries?" he teased.

"I'm not going to seduce him at all," Esther said airily. "We're friends."

"No, sis," Abe said, grabbing her hand. "You and I are friends. You look at him like he's a mountain of chocolate ice cream and you can't wait to dive in."

Esther flushed, disconcerted. "Really?"

"What's wrong with that? You aren't the kind of woman who ought to be spending her life alone."

"Abe," she protested. "Stop matchmaking me." She pulled her hand free and picked up the net bag, deciding to finish her accounting in the morning. "I won't lie to you—"

He chuckled. "You're incapable of lying."

Esther shook her head. "I'm just not ready for anything intense." She pursed her lips thoughtfully. "And I don't think there's any other way for me to conduct a relationship." Briskly she turned away and lifted the Closed sign into place.

"At least you've got me," he said, tongue-in-cheek.

"Some comfort!" She rolled her eyes for emphasis.

He reached for a strawberry. "Least I'm not as ugly as you are—sheesh!" He popped the berry into his mouth. "You'd make a freight train take a gravel road."

Esther moaned at the return to childhood, when Abe's favorite name for her had been "Gunboats," because her feet had grown so much faster than the rest of her. Gathering the bag of groceries, she headed for the kitchen. "But you have to sneak up on a glass of water to get a drink!" she called over her shoulder.

Abe followed her. "But they had to tie a bone around your neck to get the dog to play with you."

In the kitchen, Esther smiled as she pulled out the makings of sandwiches for Abe. She'd lose the game—she could never remember or make up as many insults as he could. Exasperated, she rolled her eyes. "Make the sandwiches."

"I'm not going to eat any of 'em," he said, eyeing the pile of sweets. "Are you?"

"Yes." She pointed. "Work!"

He grinned impishly. "Yes, ma'am."

"Stop teasing me now. I am going to take a shower and put on my grown-up self, so you behave yourself."

"I'll do my best."

As she climbed the back stairs, he called, "Esther!"

"Hmm?"

"I know you guys are friends, but how about that blue dress?"

She wrinkled her nose. "I'm too fat to wear that dress."

He shook his head and disappeared, muttering, "Women!"

Indeed, thought Esther. What about *men?*

Alexander carried a bundle of freshly cut irises from his garden back to Esther's in the warm, late afternoon. In a long brown bag was a loaf of French bread and a bottle of white wine.

He felt extraordinarily aware and alive today, as if all of his senses had been half sleeping and now stretched, awake and refreshed. Thick bands of gold light bronzed the air, and violet shadows fell from the trees to the grass. Against the western sky the mountains stood sentinel, like soldiers in rough blue wool. The sidewalk warmed the soles of his shoes and a soft wind fluttered by, smelling of pine.

Rather than ringing Esther's bell when he came upon her house, he followed the sidewalk toward the backyard. Here the light was thicker still, and a scattering of wrens picked through the soil of the herb garden. As Alexander stepped into their realm, they flapped into a tree, whistling in alarm and worry.

He settled the irises on the table and opened the waxed paper covering the bread, then broke off pieces and tossed them toward the garden. In unison, six small gray heads quirked; a dozen tiny black eyes looked at the offering. He chuckled to himself.

From behind him, Abe said, "You like birds, Alexander?"

"Oh, I don't know." He shrugged and glanced over his shoulder. "They just always seem to be so much at the mercy of everything."

Abe flashed a crooked grin, munching cheerfully on a banana. "Esther told me about your pirate cat."

"He's a pirate, all right." Abe had carried out a glass bucket of ice and a platter of sandwiches, covered against the air. "Can I do anything to help?" Alexander asked.

"Esther's finishing the fondue in the kitchen. You might be able to help her lug some of the stuff out."

"Gladly." He gathered the flowers, leaving the bread on the round wooden table, and went inside.

In the dimness of the kitchen, he paused momentarily. As his eyes adjusted, he saw Esther standing over the counter, piling strawberries into a bowl. Diffused north light poured in through the window and washed over her. The pale red hair was caught back in a black velvet ribbon and her head was bent over her task. In the old-fashioned kitchen, with ferns and ivies spilling from the windowsills, she looked like a painting of a woman in the middle ages—there was that fullness and richness about her figure and the simple contentment she radiated.

For the first time, she wore something ordinary, a blue tank-top sort of dress that left her arms bare and clung to her curves. Alexander felt himself grow hot as he looked at her, his heightened senses whirling at the smell of chocolate and irises, at the delightfully beautiful woman in her serene kitchen. As he watched, she took a strawberry from the bowl and put it into her mouth, and a single bead of silvery water clung to her lower lip.

He must have made some sound, for she turned. "Alexander!" she said, her voice honeyed with pleasure. "What beautiful flowers."

He gave her a mock bow and raised an eyebrow. "For the loveliest lady in the kingdom."

She smiled, her eyes glowing as she accepted them. Bending her head into the velvety petals, she inhaled their scent, then closed her eyes and very slowly moved her chin and cheek and nose over the flowers in an unselfconsciously sensual gesture. "Thank you."

He stepped closer, drawn against his will. Taking her free hand, he lifted it to his lips, allowing himself to taste the heat and silkiness of her flesh for an instant before he let her go. "It was my pleasure."

"How gallant you are," she said, flashing her inviting smile. "Perhaps I should call you Lancelot instead of Alexander!"

"Traitor's name!" he protested jovially.

"Ahh." The word was a sigh. "Then you must be Arthur himself. I should have known it."

He smiled, enjoying himself. "And what would lead you to such a conclusion?"

A hint of color touched her cheeks and she lowered her eyes for a moment. He wondered how such a vitally sensual woman could have learned to be shy and thought again that her ex-husband must have been a fool.

It was an impression that was trebled when Esther lifted her deep brown eyes. A sparkle of humor and passion shimmered there as she said, "You just have a kingly way," she teased.

He stepped closer. Above the heady mixture of chocolate and irises, he could smell Esther herself now, a soft scent of lavender. Deliberately, he let his eyes skim the scoop neck of her dress, where a luscious swell of breasts peeked out. "I seem to remember Esther is the name of a queen," he said quietly.

"So it is." She didn't draw back this time. Instead, a throaty chuckle escaped her throat at some private vision. "I have to get these flowers in water," she said and slipped away from him.

Alexander watched her at the sink, admiring the fullness of her hips and the dip of her waist, aware that he was deeply aroused by simply talking with the glorious Esther. "I'll carry these outside, shall I?" he said, picking up bowls of strawberries and chunks of watermelon.

The meal, as far as Alexander was concerned, was equal parts heaven and hell. The sandwiches went ignored as they all helped themselves to chunks of pears and watermelon, bits of cheese and bread, sips of the crisp wine. Around them, birds twittered and insects zoomed through on busy errands.

"Not bad, huh?" Abe said, dipping a slice of apple into the common pot of chocolate.

"It's delicious," Alexander agreed. "I gather it's something of a tradition?"

Esther laughed, the sound as golden as the thick, late light. "*Food* is our tradition." She idly lifted a small triangle of watermelon and flicked the visible seeds away with a finger. "No one on the block could eat as much as we could."

"You have to understand," Abe cut in, "that the lovely lady you see before you grew eight inches in a single year." He chuckled. "Four more in her feet."

"And he grew *ten,*" Esther said, slapping his arm. "*Twelve* in his feet."

Alexander chuckled at their teasing. He'd not been quite certain of their relationship at first. Now it was plain they were very close, but like siblings. He shifted his gaze to Esther, admiring without urgency the tendrils of blazing hair against her cheek.

She caught his gaze. "What were you like at fourteen, Alexander?"

"I can barely remember fourteen," he said with a frown. Suddenly he did remember. "Ah. Grammar school. My best friend was James Dervish and we used to go to movies to try to pick up girls."

"Without any luck, I bet," Abe put in.

"Abe!" Esther protested.

"Hey, I was fourteen once, remember?" He glanced at Alexander. "The ones you like always had—" he cleared his throat "—outrageous figures and a lot of eyeliner, and they wouldn't give you the time of day for a hundred bucks."

"We must have gone to the same movies," Alexander said with a laugh.

"Me and my girlfriend Judith were the skinny girls in the balcony, trying to get the big boys' attention," Esther said.

"Until Judith bloomed," Abe said with a chortle.

Esther cocked her head, smiling. "That's when I took to horror novels. You can't go to the movies alone, after all."

"Horror novels?" Alexander echoed.

Esther held back a smile, her sleepy eyes glittering with humor. "My secret addiction," she said.

"Do you mean *Frankenstein* and *Dracula,* that sort of thing?"

"Well, back then, I had to make do a lot with those creepy comic books—you know, *Tales from the Crypt* and *Eerie Tales.*"

Alexander had a vision of a thin, young Esther, hair in pigtails, wiling the summer away with gore-splashed comic books. He chuckled. "And now?"

"There still aren't many good ghost stories, unfortunately, but there's almost anything else. It's practically a horror renaissance." She shrugged, as if feeling a little defensive. "It's not for everyone, I admit."

"My mother loved ghost stories," Alexander said, taking up another strawberry. "One of her favorites was *The Haunting of Hill House.*"

"Oh, that's a wonderful book!" Esther leaned forward eagerly. "Have you ever seen the movie? It's terrifying!" She shuddered for effect. "There's a scene where the woman reaches out to hold hands with her friend, while this child is crying and crying and crying... and when it's over, she looks down and she is holding hands with nothing. It's great!"

Abe shook his head. "You're one sick puppy, Esther Lucas. Horror novels." He looked at Alexander. "What do you read?"

Comfortably he leaned back. "History, of course." He winked at Esther. "But I've got my own secret addiction to suspense and murder mysteries."

"Ha!" Esther cried, slapping Abe's shoulder playfully. "See? You're the only stuffed shirt around here."

"America," Abe pronounced in an exaggeratedly droll voice, with a shake of his head. "In thirty years, literary fiction will be dead, killed by indifference." But he smiled as he said it, and Alexander realized it was another long-standing argument between them.

"I'm too stuffed to debate with you," Esther said with a sigh. "And it's much too nice an evening. I just let you screen out all the boring stuff so that I don't have to waste my time."

Alexander smiled, then excused himself for a moment.

Although they had all been laughing and talking through the meal, by the time the sun had dropped to shine like an impaled ball on the points of the mountains, Esther noticed the lines of strain around Abe's mouth. She waited until Alexander stepped inside for a moment, then touched her friend's hand. "You don't look well."

He managed a wry grin. "Trying to get rid of me?"

"You know better." She squeezed his hand. "And I know you too well to be fooled by that brave expression. If you've had a bad week, you'd best get home and get to bed."

"I guess I should," he said without enthusiasm. His dark eyes fixed on the horizon and Esther saw the loneliness in them.

"Why don't you stay here tonight?" she suggested. "You can sleep in one of the boy's beds and in the morning, we'll have brunch."

"You always see right through me," he said. "I've been stuck in that apartment a lot lately." He stood up stiffly and kissed her head affectionately. "Thanks for the offer. Does it matter which bed and can I go up right now?"

"I'll come up with you."

"Nah." The answer was firm. "I'll find my own way." He gave her a wink. "I'll see you in the morning."

He disappeared inside and Esther picked up her glass of wine reflectively. Through the pale amber liquid, the herb gardens were a blur of leaves and paths, as inviting as an Impressionist painting. The sun sank abruptly behind a mountain peak and the world was plunged into a pale purple dusk. She sighed, sated with food and quiet and good company.

So when Alexander noiselessly joined her, she looked at him comfortably, at ease with him in a way she hadn't been before tonight.

"Are those your herb gardens?" he asked, gesturing.

"Yes. Would you like to see them?"

"Will you tell me all their magical properties?" he asked with a quirk of his lips. "Or is that sacred wisdom, passed only into the hands of women?"

Esther stood, cocking her head as if in serious consideration. "Well, if men had not overtaken the medical establishment with such bluster, they'd have had this knowledge themselves." At the edge of the garden, she slipped off her sandals and glanced over her shoulder at Alexander. "Since you are simply a good man of letters, I suppose I won't be shattering any secret trust."

"Is it holy ground?"

"Pardon me?"

He pointed to her bare feet. "Shall I remove my shoes in order to walk more gently upon holy ground?"

"Oh!" She laughed. "I don't know why I always take them off. I guess I just like the way the earth feels. You can leave yours on."

But he'd already bent to remove them, shedding his socks as well. At the sight of his naked white toes, Esther felt a surge of orange hunger race through her body. She stared at his feet for an instant, taking in the high graceful arches and tapering shape, wondering with some dimly logical portion of her brain why bare feet should create such a reaction. Flustered, she let her eyes travel over his legs and chest, finally reaching his face, which was aglow with amusement. "Didn't expect that, did you?"

"No." She smiled softly. "You often surprise me."

"Good." He lifted that devilish eyebrow.

There was nothing much to say to that, so Esther turned and led the way over a narrow path through beds of apple-scented chamomile and heady sweet marjoram. "Herbs aren't showy," she said. Bending over, she plucked a spray of thyme, its stem dotted with tiny pale flowers, and handed it to him. "But they have their rewards. Smell."

He obligingly held the spray to his nose. "Mmm—spaghetti."

She rolled her eyes. "How romantic of you." But she laughed and led him farther down the paths that circled the dense stands of herbs.

"This," she said, stopping before a round bed filled with small, dense shrubs of silvery green, "is my pride and joy."

Alexander paused, still twirling the thyme between his fingers. "And what is it?"

Esther bent in the gathering twilight, feeling a magical mood overtake her. Surrounded with gray light and the mingled perfumes of her herbs, she felt suddenly a little tipsy in spite of the fact that she'd only drunk a single glass of wine.

Kneeling in the cool earth by the plants, she reached out and gently bruised a stalk of lavender between her palms, covering her hands with the precious aromatic oil. She stood up again.

With a slow smile at Alexander, she rubbed her open palms over her neck and chest. "Lavender," she said quietly. She tilted her head, and feeling dizzy at her boldness, added huskily, "Smell."

His eyes darkened and he stepped forward, one hand settling around her waist in a light touch. Esther felt her breath quicken as he bent his curly head over her shoulder. His nose touched her skin just below her ear. "Mmm," he rumbled. "It smells of night."

She felt his beard move over the curve of her shoulder, and his lips touched her neck lightly. Esther sucked in a breath, feeling a tingle travel through her breasts and belly and loins. She reached up to grasp his arm as he continued his exploration, his mouth traveling downward along her neck to land on her collarbone. "It smells like stars," he whispered, and moved against her, his body lean and hard against her softer curves.

Esther felt suspended in time as the gray light of evening deepened. A hush settled over the garden. She was aware only of Alexander's teasing lips and the gentle scratch of his beard along her flesh. She felt deliciously aroused and yet perfectly safe.

But then he opened his mouth and settled his hot tongue in the hollow of her throat. At the same instant, his bared foot brushed over hers. She gripped his muscled arm fiercely.

The kiss the night before had been one of gentle exploration, a kiss of lips and introduction. This was nothing like that. Alexander pulled her roughly against him, pressing their bodies hard together as his mouth found hers, taking it with fervor. His tongue sizzled along the edges of her mouth, teasing and flicking to gain entrance to the heated cavern of her mouth. With a small, helpless moan, Esther opened to him, her hips going weak as he slanted his mouth over hers.

And yet for all the passion of this kiss, his skill was no less exacting now than it had been the night before. He suckled her lips and teased the tip of her tongue with the tip of his before plunging. Then he retreated and began again. His hands traveled over her back, skimming the upper rise of her hips, then explored her sides, up to her shoulders.

Esther lost herself in the glory of him, in the riotous feel of his curls clinging to her fingers, in the hard wall of his chest against the aching rise of her breasts, in the heat emanating from his body as he pressed into her urgently. He tasted of chocolate and wine and strawberries. She moved against him in unconscious invitation.

When his hands began to explore the outer swell of her breasts, Esther came with a sudden crash to her senses. They were in her garden, she thought with embarrassment, and broke away from him urgently.

For an instant, they stared at each other in stunned silence. His hair was mussed by her fingers and his changeable eyes were a dark, vivid turquoise. Her lips felt bruised, her knees shaky, and her body burned with his imprint. Shocked at the invitation she had issued—especially in light of the fact that she took great pains to avoid giving the wrong impression to men— she turned away, flushing painfully, and crossed her arms over her chest protectively. "I don't know what got into me," she said quietly. "I'm sorry."

Alexander growled in frustration and touched her shoulder. "Look at me."

She squeezed her eyes shut, keeping her head bent, remembering the wanton way she had moved against him, the provocative way she had rubbed lavender oil over her neck and chest. "I can't," she whispered.

He put his palms on her shoulders. "Esther."

When she still would not turn, he let go of her. "All right. When you're ready, we'll talk."

She knew her manners were horrible, that she ought to turn and tell him she had enjoyed his company, but when she'd been ready to tear her clothes off for him and make love amid the herbs, polite pleasantries seemed a bit absurd. She kept her face resolutely turned away, imagining over and over her hands reaching up to cover her flesh with lavender oil, then cocking her head . . .

From the deep closet of her mind where the memories of her failed marriage were stored, she heard another voice, annoyed and tired: *Damn, Esther, all you ever want to do is jump into the sack.*

As she listened to the whispering sounds of Alexander retreating through the garden, she ached at that old voice and the shame it made her feel. Intellectually she knew John had been lashing out at her to cover the guilt he felt over his inability to remain faithful to her. Emotionally—well, emotions were always harder.

Alexander's voice reached her over the grass. "Good night, Esther."

She couldn't let him leave on this note, she thought wildly. Abruptly she turned. "Alexander," she said on a note of entreaty.

He waited.

But she had no idea of what she wanted to say. "I'll see you on Tuesday," she said.

"Tuesday it is," he replied.

Esther watched him go with a sinking feeling. This had all been a mistake, she thought. A great big mistake.

Chapter Five

Alexander bolted awake in the dead still of the middle of the night. Next to him, Piwacket glared at having been disturbed, but settled back down as Alexander got up.

He'd been dreaming of Esther. Not in any of the typically male ways his mind ordinarily conjured up in these circumstances. Instead, he'd dreamed of her standing on a rocky cliff overlooking the sea off the coast of England, her arms stretched out in jubilant celebration, her pale red hair tossing on a wild sea wind. It was night in his dream. A full moon gave her bare white shoulders a pearlescent wash and the wind pressed her dress against her lush, round figure.

Staring out the window of his bedroom to the sleeping landscape, he had to smile at his imagination. Almost equal measures of Maxfield Parrish and

Guinevere—a vision of Esther brimming with power and holy strength.

He frowned. Not Guinevere, he decided—or a Maxfield Parrish painting, for that matter. Both were too wispy, too ethereal, too vague to be the robustly drawn Esther.

Again the dream flashed in his mind—the tossing sea and her lush figure, the bright moon glowing in the sky as if to illuminate the source of all womanly power....

He remembered her kiss in the garden, the flash of sensual heat in her eyes as she lazily opened her palms to spread lavender oil over her flesh, then casually, teasingly, offered the long white neck to him. He'd gone to her easily, his senses hungry for the taste and feel of her.

But the passion that had exploded within him at the taste of that smooth skin had stunned him. And when his tongue had found the hollow of her throat, he'd seen her nipples bud into taut, eager points below her dress, evidence of her own desire.

He'd been so instantly, vigorously aroused that he had worried he would frighten her away. Instead, she'd received him as naturally as if he were the rain and she a thirsty stand of lavender.

Even now, hours later, the memory of her luxuriant form cushioned against the hard angles of his own was enough to arouse him virulently.

Fleeting, lusty liaisons had never been his style. Like all men, he'd certainly experienced his share of wild hungers, but he'd found his mind, as well as his body, had to be engaged. Susan had been his match intellectually as well as physically and he had supposed that he was lucky to have found it once in his lifetime.

Yet in less than a month's time, Esther had completely captivated him. He wanted her with a force that put any previous acquaintance with the word to shame—wanted her in his bed for weeks of nights spent tumbling and tangled, days spent resting for the night to follow. An aura of erotic promise surrounded her as completely and naturally as her red hair and smooth pale skin.

God help him.

For if it had been only that allure, he might have indulged the wish. Few men, after all, could contemplate that ripeness without seriously considering seduction at some point or other.

Tonight, he'd realized her effect upon him was deeper than the volatile chemistry between them. She intrigued him, made him laugh, took nothing too seriously.

He'd also learned she was not comfortable with her sensual nature, at least where it concerned men. For that reason alone, if no other, he couldn't run the risk of hurting her in an affair based on passion that would burn itself out eventually.

Piwacket jumped from the bed to curl around Alexander's feet, meowing in hopes of a midnight feeding. He glanced down distractedly as he considered the problem. No one with the exuberance she displayed should have to hide her true nature. It was practically a crime against nature.

For it was Esther's complete adoration of the moment at hand that made her so irresistible. Whether it was hugging the body of a child or watching a karate match or admiring a rose, the instant in time that she occupied received her complete and undivided attention. It was a rare quality.

He smiled to himself, thinking how much his students would like her. Somehow, he would find a way to free the Esther within before she traveled on her way.

There was danger in the task, a danger his dream of her had spelled out very clearly. The very power he sought to free might ensnare and wound him.

But as if he'd already been bewitched, a ribbon of memory unfurled against the dark of his imagination, igniting sensual memories of Esther in the sweetly scented garden. On his tongue, he tasted her lips and satin skin. His hands burned with the feel of her hair. His ears reproduced her throaty sound of pleasure.

Against the onslaught of such vivid memories, the danger seemed very small.

Tuesday morning, Abe minded the shop and her children while Esther went to class. It was a perfect solution in many ways, she thought. Abe needed to be out, to work and feel valuable, but his physical problems made it difficult for him to find work elsewhere. She was surprised she hadn't thought of asking him to fill in for her before this.

The class began at 10:30. Esther walked to the campus, steadfastly concentrating on the beauty of the early summer day rather than upon her upcoming encounter with Alexander.

After much thought, she had come to the conclusion that she could only allow herself to be friends with him. Aside from her nagging sense that he was drawn to her for the healing he needed, there was something about him that unleashed the wanton side of her nature. No matter how tempting it was, she couldn't afford to let her guard down so completely.

The truth was, she was more than a little confused by the power of her response to him, and that seemed the best reason of all to keep the relationship purely platonic.

There was no avoiding the fact that there would be some sort of relationship. She would be seeing him every Tuesday and Thursday for the next eight weeks, and besides that, she liked him. He was intelligent and clever and interesting, a puzzle she had been hankering to solve. There had been little enough of that in her life of late, and her friendship with Abe proved men and women could be simply friends.

She found the classroom, high in a building facing the quadrangle. Alexander sat on the edge of a table, one foot swinging, the other bracing his weight. For an instant, Esther paused in the hall, waiting for her heart to stop its silly thudding.

Most men dressed in a shirt and tie would look businesslike. Alexander didn't even look properly professorial. Not even crisp cotton could completely hide the hard curves of his shoulders or the nip of his lean waist. His casual pose put one thigh against the fabric of his slacks and even from across the room she should see how hard it was, how beautifully muscled. His unruly dark hair had been painstakingly brushed away from the craggy face, but already the curls were springing into their natural disorder. She longed to go in there and tousle them back to freedom.

A swelling tingle rushed through her. Maybe, she thought ruefully, she didn't want to be friends with him after all.

When he caught sight of her, standing uncertainly in the doorway, he straightened and gave her a great, welcoming smile. "Esther!" He extended a hand. "Come in."

"I'm a little early, I think," she said.

"Not much. The students will be wandering in any moment."

Esther nodded, disconcerted a little by his nearness. She could smell his cologne and imagined that the warmth of his body radiated outward to brush hers.

"Nervous?" he asked.

"About the class?" she asked, and then realized how incriminating that was. "No, not at all."

He chuckled. "It would be arrogant to assume it was myself that had you wringing your hands."

Esther finally looked at him. "Yes, it would be." Ruefully she grinned. "It would also be true." So much for playing it cool.

"Have you forgiven me, then?"

"Forgiven you?"

He touched her cheek. "For nearly ravishing you in the garden when you were so innocently showing me your herbs."

Startled, she looked into his deep blue eyes and saw no censure there, only a teasing good humor. But it didn't really matter what *he* thought. She carried enough censure for both of them. Seriously she said, "I think we should both just forget about that."

"You may, if you like," he said, dropping his hand to his lap. "But I would rather not."

A pair of students appeared at the doorway, and behind them came three more. Within a few minutes the eleven students were assembled, chattering familiarly with one another. Esther looked them over curiously, seeing nothing particularly out of the ordinary about them. Not right away.

But there was a preponderance of unironed cotton in their clothes. The girls wore little makeup and the boys seemed to favor longish haircuts. All in all, a serious, intellectual lot. Esther smiled to herself—these were the alternative radio addicts, the Greenpeace activists, the poets.

"Good morning, ladies and gentlemen," Alexander said, hands comfortably in his pockets. "Are you ready for the dark side of the dark ages?"

"You can do your best to convince us," said the youth in the front row.

Alexander flashed a twinkling eye toward Esther. "As you see, I've not undertaken the job without reinforcements. This is Esther Lucas and together we will endeavor to disabuse you radical romantics of your foolish notions." He picked up a stack of papers. "Here is your syllabus and book list. While I pass it out, I want you all to introduce yourselves to Ms. Lucas. Don't bother to announce your major. Only history majors would devote themselves to such a summer class."

"I'm Keith Martinez," said the boy in front. "I think I remember you from the Renaissance fair."

"Yeah," said another student derisively, "when the fair Keith got trounced."

"I remember," Esther said with a grin. "My children were certain you took your swords and went to fight dragons."

Appreciative laughter met this comment and Esther felt the students warm toward her. They introduced themselves one at a time, teasing and chiding one another. By the time the introductions were completed, two groans had gone up, evidently over the syllabus.

"None of that," Alexander warned, but she could swear he was taking great pleasure in their complaints. "This is an upper level seminar and the short span of time we have to meet requires a great commitment on your part. We have a lot of ground to cover."

Esther picked up the syllabus curiously. Three books were listed, but a parenthetical sentence said that they were all available in softcover editions. One research paper was required by midterm and the students would then present their findings to the others. Two exams. She raised her eyebrows.

An attachment listed the topics available for the papers and presentations. As Esther scanned it, she grinned again. Dentistry was one of the options. Hygiene and sewage was another, peasant homes and comforts yet another.

As she read, Alexander was giving his class a general overview of what they could expect and what he expected in return. Dutifully the students took notes, their banter and play forgotten.

He dismissed early and spent several minutes fielding questions and concerns afterward. Keith claimed the hygiene topic, a curious, triumphant smile on his lips.

When they had gone, Alexander closed his book and looked at Esther. "Well, what do you think?"

"I think I'd have avoided your classes, Professor."

He cocked his head. "No, you wouldn't have. You were a good student."

"How do you know? Maybe I was a party girl."

"No. You're smart and curious." He stroked his beard, measuring her. "You were one of those patchwork students, I'll wager—three A's and three C's every semester."

Esther blinked in surprise. "You're good. How can you tell?"

He raised that single, mocking eyebrow. "You threw yourself into anything that excited you and thus took the highest grade, but you also muddled through the less interesting classes."

"That was college," she said, unable to prevent a grin. "In high school, I had either A's or *F's*."

He chuckled. "How did that go over at home?"

"Not at all proper for the daughter of a colonel." She laughed wickedly. "Even if he was retired by then."

"The daughter of a colonel?" he asked. "Are you really?"

She sighed. "I really am."

"I had the impression that you and Abe had been friends for a great many years."

"We're both Army brats. Spent our childhoods in Okinawa and Germany and Fort Bliss—everyone seemed to get transferred more or less together." She sobered. "When Abe got back from Vietnam, he was sent to Fitzsimmons Hospital in Denver. My father retired in Colorado Springs."

"So that's where you went to high school?"

She grinned. "It was by design, I can tell you. My father hoped I'd fall in love with a cadet at the Air Force Academy and continue the family military history." She realized she'd spilled out her entire childhood in a few short sentences and gave him a quizzical glance. "Sorry. Didn't mean to get going like that."

His marble eyes danced with humor and a very male appreciation that flickered over her face boldly. "I don't mind."

It was time, she realized, to tell him she'd decided they should be friends only. She extended her hand. "Thank you for including me in your class, Alexander. I think I'm going to enjoy it very much."

If she had expected hurt or bewilderment at the businesslike gesture, she was disappointed. He accepted her hand, his eyes twinkling, and before she could pull it away, lifted it to his lips. But it was to her upturned palm he pressed his sensual mouth. The moist warmth of his mobile lips sent a thrill racing over her nerves. "Alexander," she protested quietly.

He lifted his head, but held her hand firmly between his own. "I'll make a bargain with you, Esther."

She waited.

"If you will agree to give us the summer to get to know each other, I promise I won't touch you."

Flushing, she protested, "It's not that I don't *like* touching you—"

"It's just a bit overwhelming."

"Yes. I have to think of my children and the greater scheme of my life... I don't have the freedom to indulge in casual affairs."

"I understand." He lowered his eyes, as if he needed to hide his thoughts, Esther realized suspiciously. When he raised them again, the color of the irises glowed a vivid turquoise. "I have avoided women since my wife died, Esther. Quite honestly," he said, raising his eyebrows, "I didn't think I'd ever want to get to know another woman."

"You don't have to tell me all of this," she said. "I'll accept your bargain."

"But I want you to know what I'm really thinking before you agree. I'm not particularly interested in a platonic friendship with you." He stepped closer, stroking her fingers. A wicked smile touched his mouth. "I'd much rather repeat the lovely episode in your garden."

Esther swallowed, feeling her heart skitter unevenly at the lure of his tall broad-shouldered body. She ached to touch his beard and tousle his laboriously tamed curls into their natural disarray, to press her lips against the high, intelligent brow. Her fingers trembled and he tightened his grip as if to soothe her.

"But I won't until you're ready." His deep voice rumbled, somehow reassuring. "I'd hate to see you run away from me simply because of the chemistry between us."

"Okay," she said in a subdued voice. Raising her eyes, she said more firmly, "I'll agree to the bargain." And then, because she couldn't resist, she lifted her free hand to his face, half smiling as she did so.

She forced herself to drop her hand and step away. He let her go. "But I will be serious about this bargain. I can't afford some wild, passionate relationship."

He grinned. "Will you sometimes allow me to hold your hand?"

"As long as you don't kiss it."

"Deal." He cocked his head toward the door. "Come let me buy you a cup of coffee in celebration."

She knew she should refuse, should go home and take over for Abe. That was an excuse. He was probably as happy as a pig in slop—his face had been beaming when he showed up this morning. "All right," she said.

They went to a small café off campus, fairly empty at this postbreakfast, prelunch hour. Alexander ordered coffee from the waitress, and remembering Esther's fondness for pastries, asked if she wanted one.

She shook her head, smiling. "As much as Abe teases me, I can't really afford to eat doughnuts whenever I feel like it. I love them, but only on Saturday mornings." She did, however, stir sugar into her coffee.

Overhead, a violin concerto played softly and Alexander, cheered by the way the morning had turned out, whistled along softly. "Bruch," he commented, naming the composer. "One of my favorites."

Esther smiled, settling more comfortably in her chair. She wore again the filmy dress with its black slip below. The autumn colors provided a perfect backdrop for her glowing hair, left free this morning to tumble in soft abundance around her face. "What I know about classical music would fit on an index card." With a teasing lift of her eyebrows, she admitted, "It was another thing my father thought I ought to know."

"Ah—so you cheated yourself to spite him. I'll have to introduce you to some of my favorites."

"What makes you so sure I will like them?"

"I can't be sure." He pursed his lips, smoothing his beard, then grinned. "Perhaps you won't."

"Do you play something?"

"No. In spite of all manner of lessons, I never seemed to be able to master anything."

She let go of a robust laugh. "Me, either." Her dark eyes danced. "I took piano for three years, clarinet for two, flute for two." She ticked them off on her fingers. "Oh, and I tried to teach myself guitar, but that didn't work, either. I also had a hundred years of chorus."

"A hundred years?"

"Seemed like it. They always forced me to be an alto and I wanted to sing soprano."

He chuckled, delighted with the picture of her as a girl that was emerging. "You were quite a little hellcat, weren't you?"

A pale wash of rosy color crept over her nearly translucent skin and he knew she must hate the easy visibility of her blushes. It made him smile to himself.

"I know it must sound like that, but I wasn't." Her gaze flickered away, toward the street beyond the windows. "It's just that life is too short to waste doing things you don't enjoy."

A chill shot through Alexander's chest. Her words burned away the hazy screen of his desire and he saw the situation with brutal clarity. He'd told himself he only wished to make love to her, but his thoughts this morning had been upon the woman she was within.

You fool.

Life is too short. The words belonged to Susan, his late wife. Even before leukemia had descended to suck life from her, she'd been adamant about that particular point: *life is too short.* After she'd died, he had often thought she must have known somehow that she wouldn't have much time.

"Alexander, are you all right?" Esther asked. "Did I say something wrong?"

He shook his head slowly. "No." He met her worried gaze and tried to smile. "Someone just walked over my grave, that's all."

Although he could tell he hadn't fooled her, she teased him. "If you want to think of me as a little hellcat of a teenager, I could tell you some stories that would support it."

He glanced at his watch, then realized how rude it seemed. "I just remembered an appointment I made. Can we continue this another day?"

"Of course." She frowned. "Are you sure you're all right?"

"Yes, thank you." He gestured toward the waitress for the check, feeling slightly ill at the sudden sense of despair that marred the beautiful day. "I'm sorry to rush off like this."

"It's all right," she said and touched his arm. "I'll see you Thursday."

He nodded.

There was no appointment, a fact he was certain Esther also knew. In his office on campus a little later, Alexander stared out the multipaned window, feeling ashamed at his behavior.

Throughout the year following his wife's death, that sort of thing had happened often. He would be sitting quietly in the company of friends or enjoying a card game, and without warning, that bleak sense of despair would fall upon him with suffocating power. Overcome with a sense of helpless rage and sorrow, he would be forced to excuse himself in haste. Running either to the dojo or to the safety of his office, he would work until the mood passed. It sometimes took days, sometimes only a few hours.

But sometimes, in the grip of that horrible grief, he'd often wished himself dead.

It had not happened in a long time, and as soon as he'd left Esther this morning, it eased away. Now, staring down at the waving green of trees outside the window, he felt compelled to understand what had brought it on.

Fear. Fear that he was allowing Esther to penetrate long-erected walls. Fear that if he allowed that, she, too, would somehow be taken from him. He honestly didn't think he could bear a third shattering loss.

Esther's words over coffee, beyond being an echo of something Susan had said, had seemed all at once to be an omen.

A finch settled on a high branch of the oak tree and Alexander picked up his binoculars to watch it. Tiny red bands striped its eyes and it sung cheerfully, gray claws wrapped securely around a slender branch that bounced on a breeze. As he often was, Alexander was struck by the seeming helplessness of the tiny creature—so small and defenseless, at the mercy of winds and rain. It amazed him that they managed to live at all. And yet they did. He watched them, year in and year out, braving the elements, singing jubilantly to sunrises and snowstorms and thunder.

He lowered the glasses slowly and looked around his gloomy, tiny office. This past week, he'd felt like that bird, alive in spite of everything. He had no desire to hole up again like a hermit. For the first time in four years, he wanted to be a part of life, to make love and sing and eat strange things with a gloriously seductive redheaded woman.

Lowering the binoculars slowly, he narrowed his eyes. Fight or flee? Man or coward?

He'd been buried alive long enough. His fears were foolish and worse, cowardly. This time, he'd face the demons down, wrestle them out of his life.

It was time.

Chapter Six

"Okay, Jeremy," Esther said to her youngest. "Pour in the flour." When he had done so, she nodded at Daniel, who measured two teaspoons of baking powder.

"I still don't understand how it's going to work if you don't follow the recipe." Daniel pointed to the card. "It says *four* teaspoons of baking powder."

"Daddy said you don't measure anything," Jeremy added, jumping up and down in place. He spied a rubber ball on the floor under the lip of the counter and bent down to retrieve it.

"Be still, Jeremy, or I won't let you help." She measured a cup of milk and handed it to the five year old, then looked at Daniel. "The reason we put in two teaspoons of baking powder instead of four is that we live six thousand feet above sea level. If we put in four, the corn bread will rise too fast and crack."

"Oh."

Jeremy took the cup of milk, but in a typical excess of exuberance, dumped it into the bowl, splashing milk all over the counter in the process. "Jeremy," Esther said sharply. "I've told you before you have to be careful."

Undaunted, he covered his mouth, his dark eyes dancing above his hand. "Oops."

Exasperated, she frowned. "We're almost done here. I just have to stir it and put it into the pan. Go outside and play until dinner."

"Me, too?" Daniel asked plaintively. "I didn't do anything."

She gave him an egg. "This is it. Then you're finished, too." *Thank heaven.* It probably hadn't been the best idea to give a cooking lesson this evening. She was tired and a little cranky.

Unfortunately when Daniel cracked the egg on the side of the glass bowl, he hit it too hard and a dozen shards of eggshell spewed into the yellow cornmeal mix. Rattled, he dropped the rest of the shell into the bowl as well. Esther sighed loudly in frustration.

"I'm sorry, Mommy." There were tears in his voice and she looked at him in surprise.

"It's no big deal, honey." She bent down to hug him. Once again, he'd absorbed and responded to her mood, a mood Jeremy had been able to laugh away. "We all get eggshells in things sometimes," she said. "Just makes it crunchy."

He still looked uncertain and she touched his smooth, straight hair. "Mr. Wizard is on TV. Why don't you go watch him until supper is ready?"

He nodded, still subdued. Esther sighed once more and tried to pick out the worst of the eggshell in the corn bread. Her hair kept falling in her face, irritating her further, and she found a rubber band to catch it back, feeling the grime of the day all over her. It had been hot, the children had been bored most of the day in spite of the fun they'd had with Abe. Actually they had both wanted to go swimming, but since Esther had to work, it was impossible—a fact neither of them would accept. The shop had been busy, and her window fan had decided this would be its last day of operation.

Now instead of something cool and refreshing, they were going to have beans and corn bread for dinner because Esther couldn't bear to waste them. The beans had been in the Crockpot all day. They would eat them.

She washed her hands and slid the corn bread into the oven and was just about to pour a glass of ice cold lemonade when there was a knock on the back door. Abe no doubt—and he would be quite welcome tonight, even if he teased her about her bedraggled appearance.

Without bothering to take off the flour-dusted apron, she crossed the room. There, standing politely beyond the screen door, was Alexander, looking as dapper as always. Catching sight of her, he grinned. "Hello!"

For one embarrassed moment, Esther thought about telling him there was absolutely no way he could come in. Not only was she personally a mess, but the kitchen was a disaster and toys were scattered from one end of the house to the other. She couldn't remember exactly, but there was probably even a pile of laundry in front of the washing machine.

Then she decided that if he was going to really be her friend, he might as well see the real Esther. Piles of dirty dishes were hardly uncommon in her life. Giving him a smile, she opened the screen door. "Hi. Feel free to run screaming over the horrors you are about to encounter," she said dryly.

He eyed her apron and bare feet, then her hair. Grinning, he said. "Well, I haven't seen that hairstyle before, I admit."

"I forgot," she said and tugged the rubber band out.

"I tried to call, but the line was busy," he said.

Esther nodded, gesturing for him to come in. "I took it off the hook."

"Shall I come back another time?" he asked, eyes twinkling as he looked around him.

"No." She wiped the counter with a dishcloth and remembered the glass of lemonade she had promised herself. "Please stay. This has been a long day filled with nothing but the complaints of children. Adult conversation is exactly what I need." Taking two glasses from the shelf, she waved him onto a stool. "You may as well see the real me, especially since you've confessed to having an orderly life." She poured the lemonade and passed him one of the glasses. "As you can plainly see, I don't have an orderly bone in my body."

"Order is overrated." He drank deeply. "You make wonderful lemonade."

She smiled. Sitting there on her stool, looking as fresh and energetic as an ad from a Land's End catalog, he refreshed her eyes if nothing else. "Thanks." She sampled it herself—sweet and tart, thick with pulp. "Have you had dinner? Would you like to eat with us?"

"I've eaten, thank you." He cleared his throat quietly and looked at Esther with a sober expression. "I came to apologize for my behavior this morning."

Esther knew what he meant, but she gave him a small grin. "Kissing my hand like that *was* rather wicked of you."

"Oh, I'm not apologizing for that at all." Again the lusty light filled his changeable eyes. "In fact, despite your floured face, I'm rather tempted to try it again."

"Don't you dare." She narrowed her eyes. "You promised."

"So I did," he said with a mock air of defeat. A frown creased his forehead. "Esther—"

She turned away, busying herself with clearing the sink in order to run hot water. "Don't, Alexander. I think I understand."

He left his post on the stool. "Perhaps you do," he agreed, coming to stand beside her. "But I would like to tell you anyway. It's important."

She looked at him, feeling afraid somehow of what he would say—that he would reveal beyond all question how deeply he was wounded, how much he needed the healer within her who was always ready to spring to the fore. *Give me your tired, your hungry, your needy,* she thought and bit back an amused quiver of her lips. But the amusement was tempered with sobriety. Like America, she often bit off more than she could chew. "Okay," she said. "If you need to tell me, I'll listen."

"Thank you." For a moment he paused, then shoved his fingers through his untamable hair.

"My wife, Susan," he said finally, "was a very vital woman, always bustling and laughing and busy. She didn't waste a moment sulking or brooding." As if he couldn't resist talking like this without somehow touching her, he reached out to take Esther's hand. As he continued, he spoke toward her hand, his eyes downcast. "When I'd get in my moods, she always said, 'Alexander, you're going to waste a perfectly beautiful hour brooding. You'll regret it when you get to the end of your days.'"

Esther smiled at the exaggerated Irish lilt he put in the words and the attempt he made to raise his deep voice into the tenor of a woman.

"Anyway," he said, "today, when you said life is too short to do things you don't enjoy, it reminded me of Susan. I always wondered, after she died, if she knew somehow that she didn't have long."

"Maybe she did know," Esther said. The part of her that was a healer wanted to reach up and hug him to her, to extend a balm of comfort to soothe the deep sorrow she felt emanating from him like a wistful song. The part of her that was simply a woman felt a swift regret that she had never been loved so passionately by a man.

"At least she had you," she managed quietly.

He must have heard the regret in her voice, for he raised his eyes to her face. "Esther, I'm not telling you this because I want you to know how much I loved her. I did, but—" A crease furrowed the high brow. "But even she would protest the length of time I've spent pulling away from life on her account." A vivid turquoise bloomed in his eyes and he said softly, "You make me feel alive, Esther."

The woman who wanted to be loved by such a fierce and gentle lion lifted up on her bare tiptoes and pressed a kiss to his beautiful mouth. The woman who had been so deeply wounded by a man very much unlike him frowned in disapproval. *He'll never care for you in the same way,* it warned sourly. Esther ignored it. "Thank you for telling me," she said.

"You broke the agreement," he commented without releasing her hands.

She slipped away, glancing at him sideways. "I don't remember you asking for an agreement."

"Nor will I."

Daniel wandered into the kitchen. "Mommy, I'm hungry."

"It'll be ready in just a few minutes, sweetie." But the sight of him reminded her to check on Jeremy, who had been awfully quiet in the backyard for much too long. Frowning, she glanced out the kitchen window. Catching sight of him, she said, "Oh, good heavens," and headed for the door.

He had climbed the crab apple tree again, the same one from which he'd fallen two weeks before. It wasn't a particularly tall tree, but neither was it strong—and the little daredevil had climbed to a fork perhaps twenty feet off the ground. As she watched, the branch bent threateningly under his weight.

Esther resisted the urge to call his name in warning and instead ran to the tree, positioning herself so that she might have a chance to catch him if the branch broke. "Jeremy," she called gently. "Come down from there right now." She said it as if there was no reason in the world to be afraid, as if she was simply exasperated with his little adventure.

"I can't," he said, irritated. "My shoe is stuck." To illustrate, he tugged his leg. The movement sent the branch creaking and groaning.

"Don't move!" She reached down and caught the hem of her skirt between her legs, tucking the end into the waistband of her apron. Hoisting herself onto the lower branches, she climbed up after him, testing the branches as she went. In only a few seconds, she found she could reach his shoe and quickly untied the laces. "Slip your foot out," she said.

He did. "Hey! That worked pretty good—"

"We'll talk about it later. You get down now." Still working to reassure and not frighten him, she added, "It's almost time for dinner."

It was harder to get down than it was to get up, at least for Esther. Jeremy possessed the agility of a cat, and scampered down in an instant. When they were both safely on the ground, she let go of a breath, touching his dark curls. They had absorbed the heat of the afternoon sun and warmed her fingers. Esther was dangerously close to tears.

"I've warned you about that tree, haven't I, Jeremy?"

He nodded, his eyes losing their shine of adventure as he realized he'd really done it now. "What're you gonna do?"

She looked back at the tree, at the slender branch upon which he'd been standing and the great distance he would have fallen, and how—

Suddenly inspired, she said, "Stay where you are. I'll be right back."

Daniel and Alexander were watching from the back stoop. Neither of them spoke as she brushed past them, perhaps recognizing that a quiet mother was more dangerous than a noisy one.

In the kitchen, Esther grabbed a cantaloupe she'd purchased that morning and took it back outside. Seeing Daniel and realizing how little he needed extra ammunition for his overactive imagination, she said, "Daniel, you wait inside. We'll eat in a minute."

"Why?"

"I'm about to give your brother an illustration, and I don't think you'll like it."

Alexander, looking at the fruit in Esther's hand, seemed to realize what she meant to do. "Come, Daniel, I'll tell you a story."

Jeremy stood at the foot of the tree, uncommonly subdued, as he had been the day he'd fallen. But it hadn't lasted, in spite of the punishment she'd given him, and she doubted a spanking would do much more. She showed him the cantaloupe. "I want you to watch this," she said, and climbed the tree. Inspired by a bicycle helmet commercial on television, she lifted the fruit to the crook in the tree where he'd been standing. "Are you watching?" she called back to her son. He looked very small, so far below her.

She dropped the fruit, feeling a little ill as it swooped by her to smash with predictable results on the hard ground below. Shakily she climbed back down. Jeremy was crouched by the split cantaloupe and she knelt next to him. "This is what could happen to your head if you fall from that high." Tears did fill her eyes now. "Do you understand?"

He looked calmly at the fruit. "Gross," he commented.

"Jeremy," she repeated. "Do you understand?"

"Yeah." He stood up and looked at the tree. "If I fall, I'll break my head wide open."

"Right."

He nodded. "Then you'd have to take me to the hospital and I wouldn't get to sleep in my own bed and they probably wouldn't even let me have my blanket."

Esther struggled with a smile. "That's right. So stay out of that tree."

"I will." He hugged her. "I love you, Mommy."

"I love you, too, baby."

It was then that she remembered the corn bread. "Oh, no! Come on."

She raced for the kitchen. Alexander and Daniel were nowhere to be seen, but a finger of carbon-scented steam curled out of the oven. Swearing mildly, Esther found a pot holder and yanked the black mass from the oven.

"Oops," said Jeremy.

Esther laughed. "I guess we weren't destined to have beans and corn bread tonight. How about a trip to the sub shop?"

"Yahoo!"

"Let's go find your brother."

Alexander sat on the front porch while Daniel showed him magic tricks. The boy was actually quite good, surprising Alexander two or three times with optical illusions and clever sleight of hand.

"One more," Daniel said, "But you have to close your eyes for a minute so I can get ready."

Alexander obliged, gently swinging himself back and forth on the porch swing. Nearby, a wren chirped cheerfully. The scent of a riotously blooming spirea bush wafted over the wooden railings and a cluster of honeybees grumbled happily to themselves over the abundance of nectar.

"I'm ready," Daniel said.

Alexander opened his eyes. Daniel's large, luminous eyes shone and he tossed an errant lock of dark hair from his forehead. Struggling to keep a straight face, he said, "I have a penny, see?"

"I see."

Daniel waved his hands, biting his lip in concentration, then held up both, palms out. "Now it's gone."

"Why, so it is."

"No," Daniel returned, shaking his head with mock puzzlement. "Here it is!" He reached over and touched Alexander's ear, pulling out the penny. "What were you doing with it in your ear?"

Delighted, Alexander chuckled. "I'll have to start calling you Merlin."

"Who's Merlin?"

"The best sorcerer that ever lived, that's who—and he'd be quite impressed with your talents."

Esther emerged from the house, Jeremy holding her hand. Her skirt was wrinkled, the hem dusty, her bare feet grass stained. All of her makeup from the morning had worn away and he could see how tired she was in the faint blue circles below her eyes. This was no young girl, he thought. A small tracing of lines showed at the corners of her eyes.

And yet, he felt a quickening in that ill-behaved portion of his anatomy. He would have liked to pull her into his lap and hold her until the weariness of the day had drained—then he would kiss her until she trembled with quite another emotion. Then, in the aftermath of passion, he would listen to the recounting of the days that had given her the character no young girl could hope to share, would share in turn the seasonings of his own days.

"Was Daniel showing you his magic tricks?" she asked with a smile.

"He said I should be called Merlin," Daniel announced.

"I hadn't thought about it before," she said seriously, "but he's exactly right." She gave Alexander a grateful look and he felt as if he'd performed a great and difficult task, rather than simply allowing himself to be entranced by a sweet, smart child. "Thank you," she said.

"It was my pleasure." He stood up. "Did you take care of your problem?"

"You must think I'm horrible," she said, lowering her eyes.

He glanced at Jeremy, who dug through the box of magic tricks with energetic curiosity. "He seems to have come through it all right," he said dryly.

"Maybe I finally got through to him." She blew a wisp of hair off her face. "Unfortunately, I also burned the corn bread for dinner. Daniel, get your things picked up. We'll walk over to the submarine shop for some sandwiches."

"All right." With a mischievous giggle, he lifted the box of tricks over his head.

"Mr. Literal," Esther said with a smile. "Put your things *away,* Daniel." She glanced at her skirt. "I guess I'd better change. Do you want to walk along with us?"

"I have another idea," he said with a smile, taking pity on her long day. "I'll take the children 'round to the shop and get your sandwiches while you treat yourself to a nice shower and a few minutes of quiet."

She shook her head. "That's very sweet—"

"Please," he cut in. "I'd like to."

"Alexander, you have no idea what you're getting yourself into."

"It's two blocks there and two blocks back."

Daniel added his voice. "We'll be good, Mom." He nudged his brother. "Won't we?"

"There, you see?" Alexander said with a smile. "We'll be fine. And," he added, "imagine how much better you'll feel by the time we get back."

The doubt in her face wavered, warring with the promise of a few blissfully quiet moments. Her full red lips quirked finally into a grin. "You win. I'll get the money."

He almost protested, but realized she would argue again. Turning to the boys, he said, "You mustn't disappoint your mother, now. She's very tired tonight, and we're going to be kind and let her relax a bit, all right?"

"We'll be good," Jeremy said. "I won't even be a raven this time."

Esther returned with the money and a list of what she wanted. "Be sure to tell them that the bologna has *nothing* on it. Just bologna and bread period."

"That's for me," Jeremy said.

"Mommy likes egg salad with everything," Daniel put in.

Alexander grinned at her. "Somehow, I'm not surprised." He tucked the list and cash into his pocket and held out his hands. "Shall we, gentlemen?"

They each took a hand. "Be good boys," Esther called behind them, "or else."

As they set off down the sidewalk, lined with spruce and elm and cottonwood trees, the two small hands tucked in his own, Alexander felt a warmth spread through him. Aside from the pleasure of the children themselves, he liked knowing he could do something physical for her. Until that moment, he'd not been aware how much he missed giving his time to another human being.

When Alexander and the boys returned from the sub shop, Esther had spread a red-checkered cloth over the grass in the backyard. Her mood was much improved, thanks to the quick but reviving shower that had washed away the grime of day. And when Alexander had no tales of horror to report, she relaxed.

They ate together in the warm evening—even Alexander, who devoured a ten-inch pepper-steak sandwich in spite of the supper he'd already eaten.

Afterward, the boys begged for a lesson in tai chi. Alexander teasingly pretended to consider their request, pulling on his beard somberly. "I don't know," he said with a mock frown. "It's a very serious thing."

"Please?" Daniel wheedled, bouncing on his knees. A smile in his eyes showed he knew he was being teased.

Alexander stood up. "All right. Take off your shoes," he said, shucking his. His fingers went to the buttons up his shirt and Esther had an instant to think, *oh, no,* before he'd shed that, too.

Her stomach flopped back and forth as she took in the sight of him, tanned and vigorous. His jeans were old and fit his long legs with almost loving closeness, showing the taut muscles of thighs and his high, firm rear end. Her eyes traveled upward over his washboard stomach and broad, golden chest, then to his face.

A slightly mocking grin met her appraisal. "Feel free," he said in a husky voice, "to join us." He glanced pointedly at her blouse.

"Very funny."

He extended a hand. "Come on. Join us. It will make you sleep well tonight."

A memory of the women sparring at the dojo flitted over her mind. She'd been wondering what it would be like to leash that power. Intrigued, she stood up.

He led them slowly through the exercises, step by step. "Grasp sparrow's tail," he said, lifting one hand, the other falling, his waist shifting.

They followed as well as they could. Esther felt a strange spell fall over her senses. His deep, accented voice was hypnotic, mesmerizing, and she felt herself moving with his words, imitating his body without self-consciousness. The exercises were difficult but somehow graceful and powerful.

"Carry tiger to mountain," he said and the boys obeyed, both of them mimicking him well.

The sun behind them lowered in the sky and a band of deep yellow light fingered Alexander. Esther paused, caught by the beauty of the picture. His dark hair fell over his forehead and his muscles rippled under tawny skin as sleekly as those of a lion in pursuit of his prey. And once again, the controlled power of the discipline exhilarated her.

Realizing she had stopped completely, she hurried to take the next position and forced herself to concentrate on what she was doing, rather than on the man who illustrated it for her.

* * *

When evening fell, both boys were drooping. "Time for bed, guys."

As she stood up, Alexander admired the smooth curve of her calves. Replete with the meal and the pleasure of the evening, it was easy to imagine simply reaching out to see if that curve was as silky as it looked. Reluctantly he stood up. "Let me help you gather all this up before I go," he said.

She looked at him quickly. "Oh, I guess it *is* getting late."

Her disappointment was unmistakable and satisfying. "Would you like me to stay?" he asked.

For a moment, he thought she would refuse. To the children, she said, "Go on inside, boys, and brush your teeth. I'll be right there." Then she raised her head and looked at him directly. "It won't take long for me to get them to bed—a quick story and prayers and I'll be back."

It occurred to him that her evenings probably stretched as empty and lonely as his own. He also realized that she had no true idea of how enticing a picture she made against the soft light of the evening, her hair gold and copper along the edge of her shoulders. Her simple peasant blouse displayed a swath of white flesh at the scoop neck and for an instant, Alexander wished heartily that he could explore again the hollow of her throat, the lovely swell of her breasts and the soft cloud of her hair.

If he stayed, he would be fighting the physical temptation she presented for every single instant. And yet, she trusted him—he would have to stick to his promise. Could he do so?

"Will you let me hold your hand?" he asked finally.

She seemed to understand exactly what he was saying. Her wide brown eyes were serious. "Yes."

And because there was so much more to her than the sheer power of her robust and beautiful form, he smiled. "I'm going to walk home and get my jacket. By the time you finish, I'll be back. How's that?"

"Fine."

Chapter Seven

Esther tucked her children safely into bed after listening to sleepily murmured prayers and checking to see that teeth had been properly brushed. As she headed back downstairs a sense of anticipation tugged her middle.

Alexander Stone.

He seemed almost too good to be true. She liked his ability to be honest with her and his easy way with the children. Often adults without children of their own mistakenly believed that their smallness of body indicated a small mind. Alexander seemed to understand that, while their young minds were still quite easily mystified and prompted toward wonder and excitement, they were quite capable of understanding ordinary conversation. Jeremy and Daniel, sensing his underlying respect, had played none of their games with him tonight.

On the landing of the stairs, she stopped to look out the window, hoping for a chance to watch him unobserved. And there he was, bent over the herb garden. She could only make out the light color of his jeans and jacket in the gathering darkness, but it was enough. He was so fantastically attractive and smart and kind. . . .

She turned away from the window, a hand pressed to her tumbling stomach. *Whoa,* she told herself— *slow down. We're going to be friends, remember?*

But for the life of her, she couldn't remember why she had thought that necessary. Men like Alexander Stone didn't come along very often, after all, and he seemed genuinely attracted to her. He said she made him feel alive.

She smiled and went to the coat closet to get a jacket. Shadows had crept through the room and she reached for the buttons that turned on the dining-room light. As she punched the On button, a pop sounded and the light burned out. Again. Annoyed at the thought of standing up on the table to reach the ten-foot ceiling in the dark, she shook her head and found a jacket by feel. A fresh light bulb could wait until morning.

As she stepped into the kitchen, she realized the coat she'd chosen was an old jean jacket she had owned since college. Oversized and worn nearly white, it was embroidered with herbs and their Latin names. She chuckled to herself—it seemed harmless enough in light of her present occupation as the owner/operator of a natural foods emporium, but it had been a gesture of rebellion in those days.

Leaving the porch light off, she joined Alexander at the picnic table. He, too, had donned a light jacket.

"It's already chilly," Esther commented as she sat down. A cool wind lifted her hair. "My mother insisted that my father take her back to Georgia a few years ago—she said cold summer nights were uncivilized."

"And you? Do you like the cool nights here?"

"Hot nights are miserable," Esther replied, thinking of Texas, where they had lived when she was in late grade school. "You can't sleep and the sheets get tangled and when you wake up, you have to start all over again."

"But what of the romance of sultry summer nights?" he teased.

Esther shrugged. "When it's that hot, who wants to get cozy with another sweaty person?"

He laughed. The sound came from deep within his broad chest, ringing into the still night like the notes of an oboe, reedy and rich. Esther realized she hadn't heard him really laugh before and was delighted to find what a unique tone there was to it. "Good point," he said, "but terribly practical."

"Believe it or not," she countered, tucking her feet beneath her skirt, "I am a very practical person."

"Is that so?" Light spilled from the kitchen window, touching half his face. Amusement lifted one side of his mouth and mustache.

"Yes, I am."

He reached over to touch the sleeve of her jacket, his index finger tracing the embroidered stem of lavender on the worn cuff. "Your manner of dress says something to the contrary."

She waved a hand. "This is a college relic and not admissible as evidence."

"What did you study?" He drew a bottle of beer from the tin bucket she'd filled with ice and she watched him twist the top and drink, wondering irrelevantly what it would feel like to have hair on her face all the time.

"Nursing," she said when he gave her a curious glance. She held out her arms to display the plethora of herbs meticulously applied. "This should tell you why I feel such sympathy with your students. It was a statement of my disapproval of the pathological approach of modern medicine."

With a quirk of his lips, he said, "And I'll wager you studied herbs to the point of saturation."

"Of course." More seriously, she said, "I was actually a very good nursing student, as well. I was within the top ten."

"So why aren't you a nurse now?"

Esther licked her lips. Like a sore tooth, the subject ached when probed and she ordinarily steered clear of it. "I met my ex-husband," she said, "in my junior year. I thought I could manage being married and going to school, but he took more time than I thought he would." Feeling as foolish as she always did, she covered her embarrassment by rounding the table for a fresh beer of her own. As she took it out of the ice, she frowned at Alexander. "I seem to always be imbibing when I'm with you. Are you a big drinker?"

He glanced at her, eyebrows raised. "Why, I don't know." He lifted the dark brown bottle to his lips, and she saw that merriment was shimmering in his eyes. "What would being a 'big drinker' entail?"

"Guess it depends," she said. "We are in Boulder, after all. Eating red meat is a pretty big infraction in some circles, but drinking seems to be acceptable—as long as you don't smoke cigarettes when you do it."

He studied her for a moment, quietly taking her measure. "I have the feeling we were talking about something else."

She sighed, standing on the edge of her foot in discomfort. "We were talking about the mess I made of things when I got married, I think."

"Why haven't you gone back, Esther?"

"I don't know." She glanced up, seeing the stars shine over the dark shadow of the mountains. Somewhere in the herb garden, a cricket mournfully chirped. "I think it would be hard to be away from my boys as much as nursing would require me to be. And I think maybe I've found what I was looking for, here in the store, with all the little things that make people feel better." She looked at him. "Here, I have all the good and none of the evil of medicine."

He shifted, reaching toward her with one long-fingered hand. "Come sit down with me," he said, his voice deep. In his eyes was something rich and kind.

She took his hand and settled next to him, feeling his thigh warm against her own. His cologne had faded, leaving behind the scent of the man himself, an elusive combination she couldn't quite pinpoint—like a streambed lined with pine needles, perhaps. His hand was much larger than her own, the fingers strong and lean, with calluses on the palms that rasped against the ones she had on her own hands. For a moment, she wished fleetingly for the elegant soft hands of a lotion model instead of her working hands with their short, sensible nails.

To her surprise, he began to gently massage the tendons and small bones in her hand as he spoke. "I think, Esther, that you still feel some sorrow over that lost nursing degree." His voice was deep in the darkness and his fingers moved over her hand, finding and releasing tiny knots of tension.

Somehow, the action dissolved her usual avoidance of the subject. She was able to respond honestly. "I loved it," she said. "I loved everything about it—the biology and the chemistry and the patients."

The pads of his fingers moved to her wrists and Esther found herself leaning back against the edge of the table, letting everything flow through her. "I adore my children and I wouldn't go back to change anything, because that would mean losing them...." She trailed off, remembering the excitement of emergency room nursing, the thrill of obstetrics, the power of surgery.

"Jeremy will be in school next year," Alexander said. "You might be able to finish then."

"No," she said, looking at his strong hands on hers, marveling at the gently aroused sensations they sent through her. "I have to support them," she said, but the words came from someplace far away, not really connected to the moment. As if she were under a strange spell, she looked at him, letting her gaze wander over the high brow and strong nose, the silky beard of mahogany and silver. She raised her eyes to his lustrous, unruly curls.

He released her hands and with one finger, touched her chin. "You mustn't let your dreams go," he said.

A husky note in his words betrayed his lack of calm and Esther looked at him with a slow smile, pleased that she was not alone in this odd, drifting sense of arousal. She steadily looked up at him, feeling his finger trace the line of her jaw and move over her cheek. Sitting so close to him in the quiet darkness, she was aware of how much bigger he was than she, his chest and shoulders broad and sturdy, his legs longer, his head above hers.

When his hand moved to her hair, his fingers threading through it, lightly brushing her scalp, she closed her eyes. And she felt no surprise when his lips danced over her lids, whispered along her lashes, his breath sending a tiny stream of heat over her forehead, his beard tickling her cheek and nose. A shiver crawled over her spine at the lush mingling of sensations and she smiled softly. "Alexander," she murmured, eyes still closed as he pressed his mouth to the center of her forehead, "you really are almost impossible to resist."

He drew back, his hand trailing over her cheek before it fell away. "That is my intention," he said with a wicked smile.

It would have been ridiculous to draw away now in fear. The last thing she felt was afraid. She let herself smile once more. "Tsk, tsk," she said, leaning on one arm in an unconsciously provocative pose. "So much for promises."

"You, dear lady," he said, gripping her face between his fists, "are a temptress that would drive any sane man out of his mind. And before I am further tempted—" he dropped his hands and stood up "—I'm going to take my leave of you."

Esther laughed, then stood up with him. "I'll walk you around," she said.

"No, I'll find my way." He inclined his head. "Thank you for a lovely evening."

"The pleasure was mine," she said, flexing her hands teasingly. Then, dropping the bantering tone, she said, "Really, Alexander, you were wonderful with my children tonight. Thank you."

"I found them easy to be wonderful with. How long has Daniel been practicing his magic?"

"A long time. Abe taught him a card trick when he was about four, and he's been obsessed ever since." The talk of magic brought back a memory of standing in the tree, dropping the cantaloupe to the ground. "Alexander, I hope you don't think I was too awful with Jeremy. I know it seemed dramatic—"

"You forget I was here the day he fell from the tree before." He touched her hand lightly, then took it away. "He's a bit of a daredevil, isn't he?"

"That's an understatement." She looked at the tree, feeling a sick swoop of *what if?* "I'm terrified he's going to get himself killed one of these days by just not paying attention. I don't think I could stand it if something happened to either one of them."

"You'd be surprised," he said in a grim tone.

"No." She looked at him. He'd lost both his mother and his wife in untimely ways and that gave him some insight into grief and loss. How could she explain the difference one felt toward a child? "It isn't the same, Alexander," she said finally, realizing there was no possible way to put it into words. To close the gloomy topic, she added, "Anyway, I think he got the message about the tree."

"I'm glad." He touched her arm. "I'll see you Thursday."

"The first lecture from the scary Dr. Stone. I wouldn't miss it for the world."

"Good night, Esther."

"Good night, Alexander," she said, mocking his formal tone.

"Wicked wench," he said over his shoulder.

Esther laughed throatily, watching him walk away until the night swallowed him. Even then, she stood there a long time, staring up at the sky full of stars, feeling full and warm and deliciously infatuated.

By long-standing tradition, Esther met her friend Melissa Thursday evening, a habit born when they had worked together in an herb store in downtown Boulder together four years before. Esther had been newly separated, though not yet divorced. Melissa had been finishing her doctorate in library science and had recently left a man she'd failed to change in ten years. The infamous Jesse was a wanderer, and Melissa had wanted to settle down.

Tonight, Esther pushed open the glass door to a small upscale café and felt her lips twist wryly. She wondered if anyone in the place was below thirty—or over fifty.

Worse, it was recently reviewed in the *Daily Camera* who gave the nouvelle cuisine high marks, the service and wine list even better scores.

Joining Melissa at a small, exquisitely appointed table, she grinned. "We're quickly becoming clichés, dear heart."

"There's no law that says you have to remain in a state of rebellion your entire life, Esther Lucas."

"Who's rebelling?" With a wave of her hand, she indicated the clientele. "This is—" Words failed her and she simply rolled her eyes.

Melissa grinned in acknowledgement of Esther's unspoken commentary. But in spite of the hip-length black hair that she wore in a single braid down her back, Melissa blended right in. Exquisitely ethnic with almond black eyes, a graceful sweep of cheekbone and dark honey skin, she was fabulously thin, elegantly dressed in a batik cotton dress and simple sandals. "Okay, next time it's pizza. Indulge me tonight. I wanted crepes." She stubbed out a cigarette—her own form of rebellion. "So tell me everything."

"We haven't even ordered," Esther protested, feeling an unusual sense of reticence overtake her. There was little Melissa didn't know about her, but Esther found she was unwilling to share anything having to do with Alexander. It was too new. "There isn't much to tell, anyway." She picked up the menu. "You start."

"I know this game," Melissa countered. "I'll tell you everything and then you'll hem and haw and tell me nothing."

"There's nothing to tell. I'm helping him with his class—that's about it."

Melissa narrowed her eyes. "There's never anything to tell when it's important to you." With a teasing shake of her head, she leaned over the table. "I'm supposed to be the stoic one here, all right?"

"I forgot." She touched her head with the tips of her fingers, then took a breath and blew it out. "He's really scary, Melissa."

"Scary how?"

Esther glanced at a vase on the table, a single Calla lily with statice. Critically she thought they ought to have left out the statice, then realized the thought was a dodge, a way to avoid thinking of Alexander. Because every time she called up a vision of his changeable, twinkling eyes or his boldly sculpted face or the woodwind notes of his laughter—

"I can't breathe," she told Melissa. "Sometimes when he's talking to me, I just forget or something, and then I have to stop and take a long breath." She met her friend's gaze. "Isn't that silly?"

"No." Melissa touched her hand.

To cover her embarrassment, Esther lifted her water glass and took a sip. She put it back down carefully and with a finger, joined the circles of condensation on the glass. "It's really nothing right now. We're just friends."

"Doesn't sound like friendship."

Esther looked at her. "It has to be," she said definitely.

Melissa knew her well enough to take the hint. "Okay. Just one question."

"What?"

"You aren't playing Florence Nightingale, are you?" She frowned. "Abe told me a little about him."

"No." She fingered the cloth napkin under her silver. "I think for once I may be the one healed."

"You look great."

"Thanks." Esther lifted her water glass, in which a slice of lemon floated. "What's the word on Jesse?"

A secretive expression flitted over the shiny dark eyes. "I'd like to wait for a minute, if you don't mind. We need a bottle of wine for that."

"Hmm. Sounds interesting." But she waited while the waitress took their order, talking about the boys and the store and the class.

Finally Melissa poured each of them a glass of delicately colored white zinfandel. Ceremoniously, she lifted her fluted glass toward Esther. "I would like to propose a toast to the end of a miserable, ridiculous period of my life," she said with a rueful smile. "The famed Jesse appeared on my doorstep last night."

Esther's eyes widened. "Really? And what happened?"

"Nothing!" The sound of triumph that escaped her lips was very close to a chortle. "My heart didn't go pitty-pat, my stomach didn't flip over, my hands didn't shake—I even invited him in and talked to him for a couple of hours."

"Wonderful!" She touched Melissa's glass with her own.

"No, wait. That's not all." She squared her shoulders. "I didn't order him out of my life in a fit of tears, or beg him to tell me why he couldn't settle down. I said it was good to see him and I hoped whenever he blew through town he'd stop by."

This moment of truth had been brewing for several months—in spite of Melissa's panicked calls to Esther from time to time, her friend had finally grown weary of waiting for a man with incurable wanderlust. "How did he take it?"

Melissa sighed. "I think he wanted to cry, but of course, men don't do that. He told me he was sorry, and then he left."

"Whew!" This time they toasted in earnest. "I'm proud of you, Melissa."

"Me, too." She bit her lip. "When I was with Abe at the concert on Friday, all we did was hold hands— but I felt more good things with him than I ever did with Jesse."

"You went to a concert with Abe?"

Melissa nodded.

A flutter of worry passed through her belly and she swallowed a cool sip of wine. "I think we'd best not talk about what happens with you and Abe. I'll mother both of you to death."

Melissa touched her hand over the table. "Don't worry, Esther."

There was something so strong and sure in her voice that Esther nodded. "Okay." She smiled to herself. And she'd been thinking that the great improvement in Abe's outlook had been due to the fact that he'd been working in the store a few times a week.

When she got home later, however, Esther heard Melissa's question echoing in her mind. *You aren't playing Florence Nightingale, are you?*

She checked on her children, shed her dress in favor of a pair of sweats and brewed a cup of tea. In the blessed silence of boys abed, she drank it slowly, sitting at the kitchen table. The quiet was so welcome she didn't even turn on the radio for company.

Alexander Stone was undoubtedly wounded. But how many people reached their thirties without collecting wounds and sorrows? If she was to steer completely away from men with need of a healing touch, she'd end up an old maid.

Well, not exactly an old maid, she thought with a smile. They were generally virgins.

Restlessly she stood up and plucked a few yellowed leaves from the coleus in the window. Superimposed over the patchwork violet and green of the plant, she saw Alexander as he had been this morning in class.

He'd worn his tie of little cat faces, a bit of whimsy in his elegant attire, just as his serious, weighty lecture was laced with jokes and a gentle ribbing of students who fell prey to his word games—walking right into a trap he'd set for them. He paced the classroom, gesturing, turning, tapping the desk or the podium or a student's shoulder. As the hour had progressed, his hair, so neatly brushed into place at the beginning, had fallen into wild disarray, curls tumbling to his forehead.

Sexy, she thought now. And intelligent. And funny. What woman in her right mind could resist such a man?

It was only when she grew insecure and questioning that she even remembered that Alexander was anything but the most fascinating man she'd ever met. When she thought of him, it wasn't his wounds she conjured up. His glittering eyes, yes—and his oboe-hued laughter, his delightfully sensual lips, his ease with her children. All those things.

She hadn't given much thought to her words before speaking to Melissa, but what she'd said was true. For once, she felt as though it was her own wounds that were being healed. All the tiny rips and tears her marriage had left in her heart were magically knitting themselves up.

One of her father's pet sayings came to mind: "What's the worst that could happen?"

The bottom line. The worst. She turned away from the window and poured a second cup of tea from the kettle on the stove, sobering.

The worst? She could fall in love with him. Madly, deeply, eternally. There was something about him that intrigued and excited her in a way that no other man ever had. It was all too easy to imagine their relationship deepening, widening, spreading. She could see herself making love with him—now, and at forty and sixty and eighty—could see herself laughing with him and debating with him until they both needed canes to get around.

It was easy to imagine spending her life uncovering every corner of his soul, learning all his memories and dreams and sorrows. Too easy. With a little shock, she realized that she was already half in love with him, after only weeks of knowing him.

It was happening too fast. Too fast for her to be able to make any kind of solid judgment over the depth and breadth of his wounds, too fast for her to know whether or not he was a man like her ex-husband, who would never overcome his past.

The bottom line. If she fell in love with Alexander Stone only to find his wounds so overgrown with scar tissue that he could not return that love, it just might be the last straw for her own heart. Not that she would wither up and die—but she wouldn't be able to risk herself. Not again.

With that in mind, she reaffirmed her weakening resolve to keep the delectable Alexander at arm's length for a bit longer. No matter how much she wanted to let down her guard with him, she wouldn't. Not until she was able to gauge the extent of his injuries.

Chapter Eight

For the next several weeks, life fell into a pattern. Esther worked in the store and gardens, took the children to their karate lessons, shared lazy suppers with Melissa and Abe, who seemed to be getting along quite well, much to Esther's delight.

On Tuesdays and Thursdays, she gave a lesson on the medical practices of the dark ages or listened to Alexander's lecture. After class, he sometimes invited her to share a cup of coffee with him and often popped in at her house for a few minutes on his way home in the afternoons. He allowed the children to practice their growing skills in martial arts with him and brought a soccer ball over to teach Daniel how to use his feet more gracefully.

As the days passed, Esther felt her attraction to him growing, rather than receding as she had hoped it might. He stuck to his promise diligently, never touching her in any even faintly improper way.

It didn't matter. As he scuffled with the children in the backyard and his hair grew tousled, she longed to slip her fingers into the silky, wild curls. When he taught, she admired his quick bright mind and animated style, feeling the chills sometimes when his oboe-shaded laugh rang out over some particularly outrageous statement from a student. He laughed in an oddly robust manner, throwing back his head, his good teeth showing, his eyes crinkling up.

And sometimes, Esther would be engrossed in something and look up to find Alexander very still, studying her. The barely concealed yearning in his eyes awakened by degrees something long silent within her, but she wasn't quite brave enough to hold out her hand to him, to beckon him closer. The raw memory of herself doing just that in the herb garden still haunted her much too clearly.

One weekend when her sons were with their father, Alexander invited her to come to his house for dinner. He broiled steaks on a grill outside while Esther admired his collection of roses. A heavy bank of clouds moved in before they could eat, however, and they settled in the kitchen with bottles of ale just as rain began to fall in earnest.

Piwacket, chased inside by the storm, sprawled on the pale blue floor, his tail flicking. He glared at Esther with a malevolent yellow gaze as she ate. She ignored him at first, but after a while a part of her was piqued. Shifting in her chair, she looked right at him. "Just exactly what did I ever do to you?" she asked.

The ratty gray tail switched and he most distinctly frowned.

"I wouldn't bother," Alexander said. "He's only come this far so that he can remind me not to throw out the peas when we've finished."

Esther chuckled. "Peas?"

"He'll eat the meat scraps, too, of course, but he'll scratch your eyes out for peas."

Esther gave the cat a sidelong look. "Why is he named Piwacket?"

"It's from a children's story." He sipped his ale comfortably. "Susan taught second grade and that was a favorite of hers—it's about the tattered cat of an English junkman that leads a band of cats to take over a neighborhood." He lifted an eyebrow as he looked at the animal. "Suits him."

But in spite of the disparaging tone, Esther could see he was fond of the beast. She grinned. "Susan brought him from the hospital?"

"Not that he ever had anything to do with her." A shadow flickered over his face, then disappeared. "Do you know what he did the second day we had him?"

"Tell me."

"Dragged a snake into the bathroom while I was shaving and dropped the damned thing at my feet."

"Was it dead?"

"Very." He grimaced.

"Probably thought he was doing you a favor." Esther cocked her head. "You know, like paying his keep."

As if he knew he was the subject of their conversation, Piwacket ambled over to a more visible spot and flopped down with a heavy sigh, his torn ear twitching in annoyance as he studiously ignored them. His enormous belly rippled out in front of him. "Quite a spare tire there, old man," Esther said.

Piwacket swiveled his head and glared.

She laughed.

After dinner, Alexander gave the peas to his cat and led Esther into his comfortable living room. "I have a surprise for you," he said, and a mischievous expression crossed his face.

He picked up a rectangular plastic box—a rented movie for the VCR. As he handed it to her, he punched the buttons to turn the equipment on.

Esther glanced at the title and grinned, clasping the box to her chest. *"The Haunting,"* she sighed. "Where did you find it?"

When he turned to look at her, Esther could see that he was deeply pleased at her reception to his surprise. "At that giant place where they claim to have every movie ever made."

Just then, a huge crack of thunder rattled the windows and Esther laughed nervously. "Are you sure you're up to this on a stormy night?"

He raised a brow. "Are you going to cling to me in terror?"

Esther bit her lip, smiling, and brushed by him to put the movie into the VCR. "We'll see who's clinging to whom, Dr. Stone."

A shimmer of light flashed over his eyes. "I suppose we shall."

They sat together on the couch. Not friends, but not lovers, either. Alexander almost casually settled his arm around her shoulders and she nestled ever-so-slightly closer to him. His lean body was warm and smelled of smoke from the outdoor grill, of cologne and that subtle undernote that belonged to him alone.

"Have you ever seen this?" she asked him.

He shook his head.

As the black-and-white film unfolded, Esther reveled in the simple joy to be had in watching her favorite movie while nestled close to a man she was madly attracted to. His touch was casual, gentle, without demands, but she was aware of a seductive arousal growing softly between them, fueled by small brushes of his thigh against hers, his fingers against her shoulder, his hard chest against her arm.

A laziness spread through her, as delicious as the heavy gold light that buttered the city in late afternoon.

And yet, there was no urgency, no need to rush further. Not just yet.

The movie began to spin its spell, capturing its audience with eerie sorcery. Soon Esther found herself holding Alexander's hand tightly, and both of them leaned forward into the story, soft gasps coming from one or the other. In one scene, when the heroine tried to explain something to the others, the doors of the room were flung open violently and next to her, Alexander flinched.

She smiled in approval. No matter how cynically he professed disbelief in the legends and lore that provided the underpinning of society, there was a part of him that had been left untouched by reason.

But at the end of the film, he gave an outraged cry. "That's not right!" he protested.

Esther looked at him in surprise. "Why?"

"It's just not. There should be something else...." He frowned. "A happy ending."

"Horror stories don't always have happy endings," Esther said. "They just have to make sense."

"There ought to be a feeling of good vanquishing evil," he argued, frowning toward the blank screen as if to make the ending he wanted appear. "A sense of order restored."

"Order is restored," Esther said with a smile, taking his hand. "What else would she do, having had this utterly shattering experience?"

He looked at her, his changeable eyes almost black. "I suppose you're right," he said. "There's always the moment of truth isn't there? The moment when the hero can choose good or evil." As she watched, his irises lightened, gaining sparks of green and blue, growing lighter and lighter as he smiled. It was the first time Esther had ever seen the change occur.

"You have eerie eyes," she said with a mocking frown.

"Do I?" He raised an eyebrow.

"Yes." Again that subdued ripple of arousal rippled through her, a whisper blowing over her spine. Cocking her head, she smiled lazily. "Like a vampire."

"Mesmerizing?" And again, his irises flickered, turning nearly turquoise. How did it happen? She'd heard of it, but never seen it.

"Like a vampire," she repeated softly.

Slowly he pushed a handful of hair away from her neck. His fingers traced a spiral pattern from her ear to her shoulder. "Hmm," he said, his deep voice nearly a growl. "I do find myself with a strange need to—" he grabbed her suddenly, playfully "—bite your neck."

Somehow, he managed to be teasing, making properly vampirish noises as his teeth lightly sunk into her flesh. But at the hot touch, at the tiny nips, the slowly flickering flame that had warmed her all evening suddenly exploded. She grabbed his shoulders, her breath suddenly gone in an ache of furious, ripe hunger.

"Alexander," she finally managed in a ragged voice. To her shame, there was no hiding the rasp in her voice. When he lifted his head, she couldn't meet his eyes. She swallowed. What was wrong with her? He was only playing and she was ready to rape him. Weren't these roles somehow reversed? Wasn't it the woman who was supposed to be constantly fending off the man?

His voice, when he spoke, was gentle. "I did it again, didn't I?"

Quizzically she raised her eyes. Her vision snagged on his mouth, framed with dark and silver threads, the lips firm and full. She wanted to taste them again, explore them with her own lips—

She sighed. "It isn't you, Alexander. It's me."

He caught her chin before she could lower it. "I chased you back into your little shell, when I was really only trying to pull you out."

"You didn't do that. I did."

"Sort of." He touched her cheek with the back of his hand. "You see, I keep trying to pretend that I'm only mildly interested in your body." He smiled and small lines from years of laughing crinkled around his eyes. "I like your mind and your approach to life, but I'll tell you honestly, Esther, I don't spend my time imagining what our next debate will be."

She smiled softly, looking up at him. His eyes sobered and he moved forward, almost as if against his will. His mouth hovered millimeters away from hers, so close his beard tickled her chin when he spoke again. "There has not been a moment since I first saw you that I haven't imagined kissing every single inch of you."

As if to illustrate, he closed the tiny gap between them, pressing his mouth to hers, dropping his hands from her face in order to pull her closer to him. This time, Esther could find no resistance—she gave herself up to the glorious feel of his chest against her breasts, to the press of his thigh against her knee, to the sensation of his mouth teasing and coaxing and exploring her own. A tiny flicker of hope flared within her, that perhaps she had found a man who wouldn't feel threatened by the lusty turns of her nature. In that moment of flaring hope, she opened herself to Alexander and heard his groan of acceptance.

For one blazing instant, they sunk into each other, their tongues and mouths echoing the motions of a more intimate act. His hands roved restlessly over her shoulder and arms, and slid down over her breasts. A blistering swell of heat rose in her belly and for that long moment, they hovered on the brink of no return.

But his hand moved away, his kiss slowed, and all too quickly, he lifted his head. Esther opened her eyes, feeling somehow drugged. His curls tumbled in glossy abandon over his head, and a dark vein beat in his temple. With one finger, he traced her lips. "You are more beautiful than you know," he said quietly.

She touched his face with an open palm, feeling the silky hair of his beard, the heat of his flesh. "Thank you."

He raised a rueful eyebrow. "Now here we are, and I've broken my promise again. I'm going to try to mend this broken fence, in spite of—"

"In spite of what?" she asked and laughed throatily.

His nostrils flared. "I'd be happy to show you," he growled and there was warning in his words.

She lowered her gaze to her hands, heeding that warning.

"Come on," he said. "The rain has stopped. I'll walk you home."

Esther's heart swelled with something she didn't stop to name. As she fetched her sweater, she thought it was miraculous that he was not in either of the categories of men she had previously experienced. He didn't try to overwhelm her with physical power, assuming that the unconscious invitation she seemed to issue somehow was a real, physical invitation to sex. Nor was he the kind of man John had been—one who found her sensual nature rather distasteful, somehow unfeminine.

They walked in silence, holding hands. The night was damp and cool. A heady scent of moist earth and bruised greenery filled the air. At her door, Esther turned to him. "Thank you for everything, Alexander. The steaks and the movie—" she took a breath "—and for understanding I'm not ready yet."

"You are quite, quite welcome," he said with a smile. He touched her face. "Thank you for overlooking my lapse."

She grinned. "My pleasure."

"It's *that* smile," he said, grabbing her to kiss her. "That's the one that inflames me." He bent again, as if fighting with himself, and kissed her once more. "Good night, Esther."

This time, she wasn't mocking him. "Good night, Alexander."

* * *

The next day when John brought the children home, Esther was brewing rose-petal jelly. Hearing them at the door, she called, "Come on in. I can't stop right now or the jelly will burn."

John wandered into the kitchen alone, his cowboy boots thumping on the wooden floor. "The boys were waylaid by the neighbor kids," he said.

"As usual." She flashed him a smile. "I remember the good old days when they threw themselves at me when I'd only been gone for an hour to the grocery store." The rose-scented jelly began to bubble too vigorously and Esther turned down the flame a jot. "I have to keep stirring for five more minutes," she said. "Help yourself to a glass of lemonade."

"No, thanks. I'm fine." He cleared his throat and settled on the stool. "Before you hear it from one of the boys, I want you to know that Jeremy had an accident this weekend." He held up a hand when she paused. "Nothing serious."

"What happened?"

"He wrecked his bike." John let go of a breath and Esther momentarily stopped stirring. "I swear, Esther, I was right there, watching him to make sure he didn't get into any trouble because you warned me he's been crazy, but he got goin' real fast and bam—" he slapped his hands together to illustrate "—he smashed into the neighbor's car."

A sick swoop of horror fluttered in her belly. "Was it moving?"

"No, thank God. Jeremy just turned wrong and slammed into the rear end before he could get stopped." He rubbed his forehead with one finger. "He, uh, knocked out one of his front teeth."

"Oh, dear." She thought of the sweet, tiny teeth. "At least they aren't permanent. Did you save it?"

"Yep. Tooth Fairy brought him a dollar."

"A dollar?" She widened her eyes. "It's fifty cents around here."

"I didn't know." He cleared his throat. "I'm really sorry, Esther. I swear I was watching him, just like you said."

Seeing that he blamed himself, Esther made a face and regardless of the jelly, reached over to pat his hand. "It's not your fault." She took the wooden spoon again and sighed. "He just has no sense of caution whatsoever. He scares me to death."

"Me, too. How do we teach him?"

"An incident at a time." She gave him a weak smile. "I'll bet he won't go nuts on his bike again."

"At least not for a week or two." He shifted and gave her a sly smile. "I hear you have a new boyfriend."

"I have a new friend," Esther said. "Not that it's any of your business."

"I'm not trying to be nosy or anything. The kids really like him."

She merely nodded. "I know."

"Okay," he said cheerfully. "I can see you don't want to talk about it." He stood up, then in an uncharacteristically hesitant manner, lowered his head. "You aren't going to change your mind about the ranch, are you? Because of Jeremy and all? My dad's really looking forward to seeing them."

"I wouldn't do that—not to any of you. Believe it or not, I trust you. I wouldn't let you take them if I didn't."

"Thanks." His blue eyes were curiously vulnerable for a moment. "You don't know how much that means to me."

"Yes, I do," she said with a grin. "Just watch him around those horses."

He nodded. "So, when I come to get them two weeks from today, they'll be ready to go?"

"They'll be ready."

"Okay." He paused. "You look real good, Esther." He winked. "Have a good time with your new *friend*."

Esther raised her eyebrows and refused to respond.

Tuesday morning, Alexander sat in the back of his classroom as Esther gave the day's lesson. He had brought with him a pile of papers from another class, as he always did when she was going to teach, so that he wouldn't make her nervous. Not that she ever seemed nervous. He smiled, watching her.

The lecture today was one they had discussed the week before. In addition to herbal lore, Esther had studied obstetrics in preparation for her nursing degree and she wanted to share the grueling conditions of childbirth in the dark ages with the students. "After all," she said, "we're presenting the dark side."

He had agreed. Now she leaned on the desk casually. "We talk a lot about natural childbirth these days," she said. "And I'm aware that, particularly in places like Boulder, there are a number of home births as well, tended by midwives." With a wistful smile, she went on. "That attitude tends to romanticize what is a very sweaty, very intense—if not downright painful—process." Her smile broadened, putting the students at ease. "Still, I'm willing to bet at least two-thirds of you believe in home births. Let me see some hands.''

Every hand in the room went up. Alexander smiled to himself. As Esther pulled out her support materials, items that would draw the differences between home birth in the 1990s and the average birth of 490, he found himself concentrating less and less upon her words and more and more upon the woman herself.

A black velvet ribbon tamed the cloud of pale red hair and she wore a dress he hadn't seen although its general style was familiar. She favored the thirties and forties, sweetheart necklines and flashy buttons, or blouses that showed off her creamy shoulders. Alexander had overheard Abe teasing her once about the fact that she didn't wear jeans or shorts like other women and Esther had saucily replied that she didn't have many assets, so she showed off her shoulders. The rest could just stay decently draped.

Not many assets. Alexander never understood where women got such strange ideas about themselves. Even in the simple black gauze dress she wore this morning, her rounded figure was delicious, the hips and breasts full, her waist proportionately smaller. He'd never been accorded a glimpse of her thighs, but her calves were sleekly muscled. For an instant, he was assaulted with a memory of how giving her lush curves had felt against him Saturday night, how somnolent her exotic brown eyes had been, how ripe her lips.

Not many assets, indeed.

He bent his head over the papers, willing himself to stop devouring her so obviously. Already several of his students had given him a nudge or two, their knowing eyes full of approval. They liked Esther. They liked

Alexander. They really liked the pair of them together.

He'd intentionally waited for three days to see her again, forcing himself to give her time. He wondered now if it had been a good idea.

Because this morning as he'd showered and dressed, as he'd walked to the campus, as he'd drunk tea in his office and left crumbs for the birds on his windowsill, his mind had been full of Esther. He couldn't wait to see her this morning, hear her laughter, see her smile, watch her earnestly present her lecture in her usual sympathetic way, leading the students around to her point of view in an almost painless fashion. She was practical, he'd learned, just as she had said she was. Practical and vibrant, bright and sweet, opinionated and empathetic—she was more alive and fascinating than anyone he'd ever met. He felt as if he'd discovered an endlessly puzzling and challenging book, one overlooked by less discerning men, one that would continue to fascinate him into turning pages for all eternity.

The thought, rambling as it was, shocked him. He looked up at her, watched her lips shape words, watched her laugh in answer to a comment a student made—*all eternity*. She caught him staring and her eyes lit with a smoky passion before she looked away.

And still Alexander stared, an unsettling realization filtering through the haze of lusty thoughts he'd used to obscure the truth.

He desired her, yes—with every fiber of his being. She had only to smile to arouse him nearly to distraction. In all his life, no woman had affected him in such a way. He somehow knew that there was perfect chemistry between them physically, that when they joined, it would be something neither of them would ever forget.

But although he'd certainly caught himself more than once spinning an erotic daydream about her, those were not the only ones he'd indulged.

In the drifting moments before sleep, he sometimes imagined eating a snack with her in the quiet of a late-night kitchen. He imagined taking her to England and wanted to meet the colonel, her father.

He was, quite simply, obsessed.

There had been times when his intellectual curiosity had been so aroused by some incident in history that he would find himself reading every book and paper written on the subject, hunting down odd bits of information—gulping it all down with an urgency that had sometimes driven Susan crazy. In trying to describe the feeling to her once, he had said that he sometimes felt that if he could only get enough information, he could create something akin to a hologram in his mind. The subject would then live, and he would be able to see it from all angles, all of it.

There was a disturbing similarity in what he felt toward Esther.

And there, sitting in the bright classroom, with summer blooming beyond the windows, and the subject of his obsession laughing, Alexander felt the doom descend. His demonic memory belched forth a picture of Susan, wasted away with hollows below her eyes, too weak to even bathe herself. He remembered the perfect face of his mother in her coffin, so perfect that his youthful mind had been completely unable to grasp the reality of her death. Finally his grim imagination conjured up a picture of a lifeless Esther, the spirit within her freed, leaving behind an empty shell.

He saw himself grieving her as he had grieved his mother and Susan—utterly lost in the lightless abyss.

No.

He would not do it again, would not face it again. He would not risk loving her, risk the loss of her. As it stood, he had known deep pleasure in holding her, in kissing her. A great many hours had been spent in her lively company. But he was not in love with her. Not yet.

It might be cowardly, but God help him, he could not survive another encounter with the sucking black hole of despair that he'd known. Not again.

As the students filed out of the classroom, Esther saw Alexander stiffly bent over his papers. She frowned. There was an odd expression on his face, thunderous and intense—not quite a frown. She wove through the aisle between desks and stood before him.

"Is something wrong, Alexander? I know the discussion got a little out of hand, but I thought they seemed to be getting the point pretty well."

"Nothing's wrong," he said, briskly, and stood up. He didn't look at her. "I was woolgathering, that's all."

For an instant, Esther was reminded of the day he'd hurried away from her in the café because something she said had reminded him of Susan. "I was hoping to buy you a cup of coffee before your next class," she said and then gave him a reason to refuse. "Do you have to rush off?"

He looked at her and Esther saw that the disturbing expression was one of thinly concealed bleakness. He searched her face and she was certain he would refuse her with a small white lie. Then he raked his fingers through his hair and took a breath. "Let's go for a walk instead, shall we?"

"All right."

"I'll need to stop by my office first."

They climbed the steps side by side toward the high room. Esther felt a strange, cloying darkness emanate from him in spite of the fact that outwardly he looked exactly the same. It occurred to her that this distant Alexander was the one who'd earned his reputation for aloofness and a part of her protested— couldn't they see it was pain that made him lock himself away?

Alexander unlocked his office door and Esther heard a flutter of wings. She followed him in and saw a cluster of finches on a branch outside the open window, their heads cocked toward the crumbs yet left on the windowsill.

"Did we disturb you, little ones?" she said softly.

Alexander took a bag from a desk drawer and reached into it, pulling out a handful of birdseed. "We'll leave you in a minute," he said, the British syllables sounding more clipped than usual, as if he were holding things in so tightly that he couldn't even risk drawling a word.

Esther silently joined him. "What a serene view."

"Yes." A shadow crossed his face as he stared out over the quadrangle and she heard him take a breath. "Esther—"

"Shh." Instinctively she turned, pressing her fingers against his lips. "Don't say it."

The bleakness in his eyes burned like an unholy fire. If she didn't stop him, he would push her away in his pain, unaware that what he most needed was the warmth of a woman again in his life.

Without a thought, she took a step closer to him. Her fingers were still pressed gently against his mouth and she spread them out over the firm curve of his sensual lips. Helplessly he reached out to brush a wisp of hair from her face, his eyes following the gesture hungrily. And for just an instant, the bleakness in his eyes faded, pushed away by the familiar wash of desire.

A swell of ancient, womanly power grew in Esther's chest. She smiled slowly in invitation, moving her fingers to his cheek to urge him closer. If ever a man needed to lose himself in a kiss, this one did now.

"There's that smile," he said huskily and bent his head to her lips, touching them lightly, his fingers trailing over her jaw. A languid fever swam through her veins, slowing time, compressing all of life into this single moment.

He wrapped his arms around her and tugged her close to him. Their thighs brushed, their bellies, their chests. "God, you're beautiful," he said, and his hand circled around her neck, his thumb tipping up her chin. He caught her lower lip between his own and sucked it into his mouth, and his teeth nipped the tender flesh once before he let go to kiss her in haste and hunger. His fingers tangled in her hair and roved over her back and he clasped her bottom in his palm.

Esther heard her soul respond to the fierce petition. As his caresses intensified, she found her own hands exploring the long fluid lines of his back and his tightly muscled shoulders below the cotton shirt. She felt the shifts of his body so intimately it was almost as if he were another part of her. A soft sound of pleasure escaped her lips at the discovery.

As if he'd been awaiting the signal, he tugged her away from the window, moving backward without easing his grip until he sat on the edge of his desk. He pulled her between his legs, his mouth falling savagely to her neck and the top swell of her breasts, moving with heat over her throat and chin.

In answer, Esther pushed her hands into his hair, her body sizzling with the demanding slashes of his mouth over her. Against her thigh, his manhood was a blunt heat. A wave of sharp dizziness swept her as she thought of opening to that hidden power, offering shelter and relief and peace. "Alexander," she whispered, loosening his tie in a sudden urgency of her own. She worried free the buttons of his shirt and at last put her palms flush against the sculpted flesh of his chest. His small male nipples pricked the pads of her hands and Esther felt her breath catch in her throat, watched his chest rise and fall with the hurried breath of hunger.

In return, Alexander's hands fell upon her breasts below the gauzy cotton, his fingers and palm lifting them to gauge the soft weight as his mouth opened, hot and wet on her throat. Her fingers curled reflexively on his naked chest.

She had felt the source of all things flowing through her, had felt Alexander's need as a compelling task. But as he made a low, growling, purely male noise of hunger, she forgot all that and leaned away from him enough that his hand could free the buttons on her dress to expose the lacy black slip below. The silk barely covered her and she was glad she had worn it as his fingers roamed the open weave with a touch as light as dust motes.

Time ceased. Esther clutched his shoulders, thrilling to the dark, heady passion in his face, a passion that had utterly erased the bleakness of a few moments before. As if in slow motion, she watched him bend his broad head to pull one rigid nipple into his mouth and felt simultaneously the heat of his tongue flick over the aching point.

The dizziness spun from her head to spill through her limbs, electrifying every cell so that even the rasp of his trousers against the outside of her thigh felt gloriously sensual. She held on to him to keep from melting into a pool of heat on the floor, her breath gone, her thoughts a whirl.

Then he was kissing her again, with his unique blend of tenderness and violent hunger and his hands roamed with restless need over her body.

It was the sound of voices in the hall that tore them from the drifting plane where only the two of them existed and dropped them back in the slightly cluttered terrain of Alexander's university office. The voices swelled as they approached the closed door. Clasped together, Esther and Alexander turned as one toward the sound, their hearts beating hard, their breath still unsettled.

The voices passed, and in giddy reaction, Esther laughed weakly. Alexander pressed his face into the cushion of her breasts. "Lord, I want you, Esther." He brushed his beard back and forth over the sensitive flesh and she shuddered.

"You're turning me into a wild woman, Alexander."

There was still no sign of the bleakness as he lifted his head, only a blazing turquoise fire. "I'm glad," he said. He touched her chin and frowned. "I'm too rough with you."

"You aren't too anything, except too good for my ego. You make me feel like the sexiest woman in the world."

"You are," he whispered. He smoothed her hair away from her face, a soberness touching his mouth. "I was going to tell you I couldn't see you anymore."

"I know."

"Just knowing you has changed me, Esther." His broad palms slid over her shoulders. "It may take me a long time to work through the things being with you has brought up."

"I'm a very patient woman." She grinned and began to button his shirt. "It was part of my nurses' training."

An odd little flicker of disturbance furrowed his brow for an instant, then was gone. "I'm glad." He fixed her dress, then kissed her again. "Am I released from my promise?" he asked lightly.

She flushed, then realized how belated it was. "I was trying to protect both of us from rushing into something we weren't ready for." She looked at his broad nose and high cheekbones, at the neat, silver and mahogany beard and the full lips that gave such pleasure. Finally she met his lightning eyes. "But sometimes you have to throw caution to the wind and take what comes."

"Sometimes," he returned quietly, "it isn't a matter of choice."

In that instant, as he gently released her and shoved his fingers through his disheveled hair, Esther realized she was dangerously close to falling in love with him. She smoothed her dress and hair with her hands to give herself time to absorb the heady new knowledge, not at all sure whether it pleased or dismayed her.

Chapter Nine

That evening, still restless, Alexander headed for the dojo. The hard exercise of his warm-up served to burn off some of the pent-up energy he seemed to carry around with him lately, but he had a hard time keeping away from the tactile memory of Esther's flesh pressed against his.

A man challenged him to a sparring match and glad of the distraction, he agreed. But even the demands of physical combat didn't completely keep thoughts of Esther at bay. She had been like a magnificent, seductive goddess in his arms today. The fact that her somnolent smile had blotted out his despair was a good sign that perhaps it was beginning to lose its hold over him. And yet, something niggled at him, something that wasn't quite right.

His wandering thoughts betrayed him and his sparring partner took advantage, dropping Alexander to the mat. The man was on his first round of training and had attained a second degree black belt, but Alexander knew he should have been able to avoid the fall. He held up a hand. "Perhaps we'd be better off going again another day," he commented. "I'm not much of a partner today."

He got to his feet and they bowed, then Alexander wandered toward the wall and sat down for a few moments. Tugging reflectively upon his beard, he frowned to call up her image: standing before the mullioned window in his office, reaching up to silence him—

The niggling sense of unease clarified—she had shed her reserve in order to help him over his despair.

Damn.

She was one of the most naturally empathetic human beings he'd ever met, a natural healer. Today that empathy had told her that what Alexander needed was an old-fashioned laying on of hands. As he remembered how easily his despair had been submerged under her ministrations, he had to admit it was effective. She was a very passionate and sensual woman. When she let those instincts have free rein, she was a force to be reckoned with.

The glimpse he'd had of that inner woman today had been exquisite, enticing, inflaming. Thinking of it now, even with the sound of grunts and thuds and feet slapping against the mats as background, he was transported. He thought of the way her pink mouth had parted on a sigh of pleasure and of the strange sensation of her skin heating as they explored each other. Every inch of him tightened in hunger. He wanted to set that inner woman free, the one she hid, the one she seemed to think so shameful. He wanted

her to see how absurd it was that she should experience everything else in her life with such open-ended
absorption and yet hold back in the most sensually
pleasing pursuit available to humankind.

But if she opened herself to him only to heal him, he
didn't want it. He wanted Esther to come to him as
inflamed with passion as he had been himself this
morning. He wanted her to come to him without res-
ervation, without ulterior motive—because she wanted
him and could not bear another minute without their
joining.

He ached at the very thought, ached to bring that
moment within reach.

He stroked his beard. The promise he'd made was
now cast aside. There was nothing to stand between
them except the children. He smiled to himself. Children slept. With a sense of great anticipation, he began to reel out his plan.

Ah, Esther! he thought.

Sunday was to be the last weekend day Esther would
have with her children for a full month. In order to
wring the most possible from the day, she planned
carefully.

Saturday night, she baked cookies and brownies and
a long loaf of French bread, then rose at five to pack
bananas, oranges, apples and raisins, peanut butter
and crackers and a dozen other kinds of imperish-
ables into a backpack. From the freezer, she took
small plastic bottles of frozen juice and lemonade and
brick-solid candy bars. A carton of eggs and a pound
of bacon went on top of these in another backpack.

She showered and tied her hair back into a French
braid, then went to the children's room. Jeremy lay in

the top bunk, flat on his back, legs and arms flung out, completely secure even in sleep. In contrast, Daniel curled around a soft plush teddy bear, everything but his little nose covered by the sheet. For a moment she just watched them, smelling the sweetness of their little boy bodies.

Children had never been a part of her great life plan. Like most girls, she'd earned money baby-sitting and spent time in nurseries at church and at her mother's bridge games. But she'd never given much thought to actually bearing any of her own—it had mainly been inconceivable to think of herself as a mother. Mothers were tidy people with a firm handle on the long-term consequences of things. Not absentminded and vaguely dreamy like Esther.

And yet these small boys were the best part of her. They had focused her. She couldn't imagine her life without them, couldn't imagine how she had ever thought she wouldn't like being a mother. It somehow didn't matter that she burned the corn bread or sometimes let their hair get too long or didn't make the beds some days because she was doing something else.

A tear touched her eyes. *I'm going to miss you!* her heart cried. A month. Thirty long days without them.

Then she sniffed and wiped the tear away and bent over each one, touching first Jeremy's soft curls, then Daniel's sleek straight hair. "Time to get up, boys," she said gently. "We're going to the mountains."

Jeremy sat straight up and stretched hard. He blinked. "The mountains? Oh, boy!" He threw his arms around her. Esther's heart squeezed.

Daniel rolled over more slowly and patted her leg. "Can we go to the chipmunk place?"

"I thought we could have breakfast there, then hike up to the meadows for lunch."

Jeremy scrambled down. "Can we wade in the creek?"

"Sure." She touched Daniel's shoulder. "I've got your clothes ready downstairs."

"Is Alexander coming with us?" Daniel asked with a yawn.

"No, I just thought of this last night."

"Can we call him?"

Esther frowned. "It's pretty early. We might wake him up."

"But maybe he'd be really disappointed if we didn't even ask."

The idea was appealing. She hesitated. Did he even like hiking? The one they had planned was long. Then she thought of his ripplingly muscled thighs and the pleasure he took in physical activity of any kind.

"Please?" Daniel asked.

What would it hurt to ask him? "Okay. You two get dressed and get your teeth brushed and I'll go call him."

But as she picked up the phone in the kitchen, she felt oddly shy. What if she did awaken him? It was only seven o'clock. And really, did she want him to see her in this back-to-nature mode? There was no point to wearing makeup for a hiking trip—it smeared and wore off anyway. And although her walking shorts were loose fitting, they exposed a lot more of her legs than she ordinarily let show. On her feet were sturdy boots and thick socks.

She bit her lip. Illusion or reality—that's what it came down to. Did she want to be real with him or keep him at arm's length, a casual acquaintance?

Thinking of the things they had talked about, the way his life and hers seemed to be getting tangled, the choice was obvious—and had already been made. She dialed his number.

But it rang three times with no answer, then a fourth. Esther's heart sank in disappointment. She was about to hang up after the fifth ring when it was suddenly picked up. "Hello?"

"Alexander, this is Esther. I hope I didn't wake you."

"No. I was gardening. Is anything wrong?"

She bit her lip. "Nothing at all. I know it's short notice, but I'm calling to invite you to come with us to the mountains. We're going to have breakfast, then hike up into the meadows and have lunch." Before he could reply one way or the other, she added, "It would mean leaving within the hour, if you'd like to go."

"That sounds wonderful." There was no mistaking the hearty approval in his tone. "I'm already dressed, so I'll just walk over. Do you need anything?"

Her spirits soared, the anticipatory pleasure she had already been feeling jumping a hundred points. "I have enough food for an army. Just bring yourself."

"All right then. I'll be there in a few minutes."

They drove Esther's economy-model station wagon into the foothills and she parked in a broad graveled area. The morning sun had just begun to penetrate the quiet stands of trees as Esther adeptly lit a fire in a grate provided for picnickers, then started the bacon frying in a skillet. The boys wanted bread and she gave it to them. "Remember, you have to be calm about it."

"What are they doing?" Alexander asked as he peeled an orange.

She pointed with a spatula to a broad sandstone wall covered with holes ranging from the size of a quarter to the size of a bowling ball. "Chipmunk condominiums," she said with a grin. "It's amazing."

"You would think the number of people who come here would chase them away."

Esther flipped the bacon. "Are you kidding? They probably eat better than any other clan in a tristate area. The little scoundrels have made an art form of begging." Hearing Jeremy giggle, she looked up and pointed. "See?"

The boys sprawled on their knees in a small hollow, tossing bits of food toward three little chipmunks who chattered and scolded among themselves, their bushy tails flicking.

Alexander chewed an orange section. "Cute little devils, aren't they?"

"Adorable."

"Not quite as adorable as you are, however." He leisurely eyed her legs. "I've never seen you in anything but a skirt."

"Well, you'll have to suffer through." She lifted a slice of browned meat from the pan. "Not even I am comfortable in the mountains in a skirt."

"I'll suffer, all right." The turquoise glow in his eyes promised it was not quite the way she had intended. A shout from the boys drew his attention.

"Look!" squeaked Daniel. "Babies!"

Alexander popped another slice of orange into his mouth and ambled over to investigate. Esther watched him squat with the children, giving them each a slice of orange to toss bit by bit to the chipmunk babies. He looked utterly at home.

He always did, she thought. It was one of the things she liked about him—his ability to be comfortable in any circumstance. She grinned to herself. Somehow, he always managed to *look* exactly right, as well: in the classroom, where he wore the crisp professorial clothes that gave him such an air of distinction, in the dojo where his bare feet and *gi* lent him a mysterious aura. In her backyard in jeans, playing with the children, he gave the impression of being an energetic and cheerful father. And now, in well-worn shorts and a T-shirt that advertised an Irish pub, with a wine-colored chamois shirt thrown over the top for warmth, he looked like a man who belonged in these mountains.

Which, no doubt, he did. He seemed to do everything well. He knew wines and history and legends; how to send a man to his knees with the mysterious power of *chi* and how to tease small children to make them laugh. He could dance and laugh and kiss with equal fervor.

What would it be like to make love with him?

The thought sent a wave of heat through her middle. Hastily, she pulled the rest of the bacon out of the grease. His rich laugh floated into the still mountain morning, reedy and robust. She looked back, and her gaze lit upon his long legs, feeling her palm itch with the urge to explore the sleek, muscled length. Sunbleached hair dusted the tanned flesh, promising an intriguing mixture of textures. She wondered how those legs would feel against her own....

At that instant, she looked at his face and found him watching her, a gleam of laughter and desire mingling upon the bold features. He winked, as if in promise.

Wiping the itching palm against her hip, she cracked eggs. Get ahold of yourself, she thought, a little annoyed.

They ate breakfast on a blanket spread under the trees, then stowed the pans and extras needed only for the early meal into the car. Esther spread an herbal mixture over the boys' arms and legs to repel ticks, and coated her own legs with sunscreen. Neither of them had inherited her fair skin, but Esther had worn a long-sleeved blouse and before they started out, put a straw hat on her head.

Alexander cheerfully shouldered the heaviest of the two grown-up backpacks and the boys each carried a change of clothes in their smaller ones. Thus fortified and prepared, they started up the long path.

It took almost two hours to hike the twisting, steadily rising trail to the summit. Because of the children, they stopped often for long sips of water from canteens they each carried. Along the path, sometimes dipping out of view, sometimes running right alongside, was a cold bubbling stream, and it attracted a wide variety of animal life. Jeremy, ever fascinated by birds, found feathers of all kinds to tuck away into the pocket of his pack, while Daniel simply dreamed along, absorbing the smells and sounds of the scene. Alexander hiked easily, sometimes taking the hand of a child or squatting with one of them to admire a rock encrusted with mica or a beautiful leaf.

Esther simply walked from one moment to the next. She'd always loved the mountains. The fine light air was perfumed with the spicy scent of pines and sunwarmed earth and composting needles. Aspens fluttered shiny, coin-shaped green leaves against the breeze. Spruce and fir trees swayed graceful arms toward earth, stretching their necks toward a sky so crackling blue it seemed unreal.

By the time they reached the high meadows, they were all a little worn and ready for a snack. Esther spread a blanket amid the wildflowers close to the stream and opened the pack with the food. The boys each grabbed a banana and a handful of cookies, then shed their packs and went to wade in the shallow stream. "Don't get out of sight!" she warned.

"We won't!"

"And Jeremy, that especially means you."

Alexander dropped down beside her on the blanket, helping himself to a brownie and a half-thawed bottle of orange juice. "Not even Jeremy can drown in three inches of water."

"You'd be surprised." She peeled a banana and looked at him. "Your nose gets sunburned easily," she commented with a smile.

He touched it. "Red so soon?"

"Not terribly, but I can see that it will be. Do you want some of my sun screen?"

"Sissy stuff." He fell back on his elbows. "When you've lived with it as many years as I have, you get used to it."

She grinned. His nose was bold and straight and perfectly suited to his face. "You'd look silly with a teeny little nose."

His eyes, almost as blue as the Colorado sky, twinkled. "I suppose I would." He brushed the back of his hand against her thigh. "Just as you would look silly with bird-stick legs."

"Don't tease me about my thighs," she said lightly, tugging on the hem of her shorts. "Especially when I have expressly come to the mountains to pig out."

"I wouldn't dream of teasing you about something so delectable." His voice had dropped a hair, and with a wicked gleam in his eye, he brushed his knuckles over the side of her leg again. "In fact, I feel distinctly vampirish at the sight of that tender flesh."

"Vampires are interested in necks." She glanced toward the children to avoid his eyes.

"I feel sure that any vampire worth his salt might give consideration to this thigh," he returned.

She slapped his hand. "Quit." But she was unable to quell a chuckle.

He leaned on one elbow and stretched his hand out to circle her foot with his fingers. "You do have lovely ankles, too, you know." He winked. "The sign of a lady—trim ankles."

"Is that so?"

"Mmm." He sat up to shrug out of his chamois shirt, then reached for the hem of his black T-shirt and before Esther could blink, had shed it as well. Then as calmly as if he'd just passed out a syllabus, he stretched out on the blanket, closing his eyes.

Esther was riveted once again by his magnificent body. His arms were flung over his eyes and one knee was cocked. Her eyes wandered over his bronzed shoulders and the tight muscles of his chest, across the taut stomach, then over his worn shorts to his thighs.

Stop it. Disconcerted, she focused on the peeled banana in her hand and had to choke back laughter at the symbolism of the silly thing.

But her eyes were drawn back to Alexander, to his beard with its silver strands, and to his unruly mahogany hair and back to the powerful chest. Everything about him invited tactile exploration—and promised satisfaction.

She ate the banana without tasting it, and reached for a cookie automatically. She caught herself and sighed. It wasn't cookies she was hungry for. Rather than make a glutton of herself, she stripped off her shoes and socks and went to wade in the brook with the children, leaving Alexander to doze.

He didn't know when she got up and left exactly; he'd been drifting in the lazy warmth of the sun, his body pleasantly spent by the hike.

But he opened his eyes and she was gone. He rolled to his side and saw her playing in the creek with her boys, her discarded socks and shoes in a heap near the edge of the blanket.

Over a haze of blue and white columbines, he watched her wade upstream to a boulder in the sun. Her hair, so neatly braided this morning, had come loose. Tendrils clung to her neck and floated around her face. She brushed them away carelessly, bending to splash Jeremy lightly. The loose, gauzy blouse fell forward, affording Alexander a tantalizing glimpse of the smooth white flesh of her breasts. He shifted, feeling a sharp, familiar stir in his loins.

How long had she sat there, raking him with her eyes? For the first few moments, he'd been amused— because although he'd considered a number of other ways he might lure her into his bed, using his own rather ordinary body had not been among them. He'd pulled off his shirt because he was hot.

Esther's soft gasp came as he stretched out. Covering his eyes in feigned drowsiness, he had watched her gaze trail over his body, feeling the path she followed almost as clearly as if she had lightly combed her fingers over him. That heated somnolence had entered her eyes, a rich, sleepy seductiveness that was almost unbearably ripe.

It had pleased him deeply to be admired that way, but it was almost more than he could manage. To avoid embarrassing himself, he'd closed his eyes honestly and blocked the almost palpable feel of her gaze running over him.

He shifted again now, uncomfortably aroused. And yet, he didn't look away from her. He couldn't. Every one of her gestures, no matter how innocent, aroused him further. The throaty sound of her laughter settled in his belly. Her dancing movements through the water rippled in his chest. The glitter of sunshine in her hair made him think of the pale red mass spread over a white pillow as she beckoned him closer. The thighs she hated so desperately were firm and strong and glistened with silvery water, and he wanted to feel them strapped hard around him.

She climbed to the rounded hump of another boulder and leaned back on her arms, tipping her face toward the sun for a moment in the pure enjoyment that was so typical for her. One leg dangled gracefully over the edge of the rock and Alexander slowly followed the smooth length upward, over the hem of her loose khaki walking shorts. At her blouse, he paused. Sunlight filtered through the thin white fabric, putting her figure in acute, beautiful silhouette.

Ah, Esther, he thought, admiring her. A painfully swollen and conscienceless portion of his anatomy urged him to cross the wildflowers and pull her from her perch and drag her back to this soft blanket in the middle of a mountain field. Here, beneath the sweet heat of the sun, he would disrobe that glorious body and worship it properly, with his hands and his mouth and his tongue, until she ached the way he now did.

Somehow, he knew he would emerge a changed man, that she would flow through him like some gilded nectar, right into the marrow of his bones and the shrunken fabric of soul.

But there were, in this moment, other considerations. Soon, he promised himself. Soon.

In the meantime, a dip in a cool brook certainly couldn't hurt. With effort, he willed his body into submission, and he ambled through the ankle-high grass to the stream.

"Decided to join us?" Esther said from her perch.

Alexander touched Daniel's head. "Who can resist wading?"

"Look, Alexander." Daniel pulled his hands from the water. They were red to the wrists from the cold. In his palms were several rocks, threaded with shiny veins. "Is it gold, d'you think?"

"It could be." He glanced at Esther, who smiled. "It isn't mica."

Daniel tucked them away in the pocket of his shorts. "I'll take them to the ranch with me. My grampa'll know."

"Does he know a lot about gold?"

"Yep." The boy peered into the water. "He used to be a miner before he bought his ranch."

"My father was a miner," Alexander offered and plunged a hand below the current to snag a rosy piece of quartz.

"Did he mine gold?"

"No, I don't think so." He frowned at the rock, then looked at Daniel. "I didn't really know him, you see."

Solemn blue eyes met Alexander's. "Did he die?"

"Oh, no. He and my mother were divorced, like yours."

"I know my daddy, though. He's going to take us to grandpa's ranch for a whole month."

The sound of energetic wading alerted Alexander to Jeremy's approach, but not quite fast enough. A furious spray of water splashed over him as Jeremy sat down in the shallow stream and kicked vigorously. He quit only because he was giggling too hard to stop—a heart-warming, deep little giggle that tightened the brown tummy and crinkled his eyes. Alexander splashed him back, gently, then more vigorously as he saw that's what Jeremy wanted. Daniel ran away to the bank in protest.

"Okay!" Jeremy gasped. "Okay, okay!"

Alexander was soaked—and cooled considerably. He reached out to help Jeremy up, but as they reached the bank together, Alexander shook his head over the boy, sending a tiny shower over his body. In cheerful retaliation, Jeremy shook his curls. "I give!" Alexander protested. "Let's get something to eat." He glanced at Daniel. "You, too. Aren't you hungry?"

"I guess."

There was an unexpected coolness in his tone and Alexander frowned, then glanced at Esther. She shook her head almost imperceptibly, giving him a somehow sad lift of the eyebrows. He nodded and took Jeremy's hand, leaving Daniel alone, as he obviously wished to be.

Later, as Esther ran a sinkful of sudsy water for the picnic things, she thought that had been the only blot on an otherwise perfect day. She had given the chil-

dren quick showers and settled them on her bed upstairs to watch reruns of *Mr. Ed* and *Mork and Mindy*.
Both of them were probably out cold by now and
would sleep like rocks till morning.

She had shed her shorts for a comfortable, aging
Indian cotton skirt, and padded around barefoot, her
feet still hot from the long, long hike. The packs had
all been unloaded, the dirty clothes tossed into the
hamper, the food put away. Alexander had taken the
car, against her protests, to wash mountain dust from
it. All that was left were the plastic dishes.

Late sunlight fingered the coleus and ferns in the
windows, and absently, she gave the plants a drink,
humming an old camp song under her breath. The
mountains always gave her this lazy, sleepy sense of
well-being. Fingering the soft, patchwork violet leaf
of the coleus, she found herself amazed such color
could exist. And as so often happened, the ripe sense
of wonder spread to her own life. She was grateful to
be so strong and healthy, to have borne such bright,
beautiful boys, to live in the old house her grandfa-
ther had built.

Thank you, she thought. Overflowing with a sense
of blessedness, she gazed out the window toward the
blue mountains and let the grateful tears flow over her
cheeks. *Thank you for this day.*

Alexander came in, carrying a blanket and two
small jackets they had overlooked. "That's everything," he said.

Esther wiped her face and turned, chagrined but
amused to be caught. "Just put them on the table."

"Are you all right, Esther?" His tone was gentle.

She nodded, smiling in embarrassment. "A little too full, I think." With a small sigh, she looked at him. "The boys are going to be gone for a month."

"And you'll miss them."

"Yes." She turned away from the plant and slipped on her rubber gloves, an oddly fussy habit she'd developed as a young girl, loathe to wash dishes. "But they'll have a wonderful time. It's important to let them go."

Alexander came to stand beside her. "I'm sorry about my little gaffe with Daniel this afternoon."

"It isn't your fault." She washed a handful of red plastic forks. "Jeremy doesn't remember what it was like to have his daddy live in the house with us. Daniel does—and he still harbors a lot of hope that one day we'll all live together again." She looked at him. "Did you ever spin those fantasies as a child?"

He settled against the counter, crossing his long, tanned legs at the ankle. "No. Like Jeremy, I was too young when my father left to remember him. And my mother, for all her eccentricities, made it seem as if it were perfectly normal for the two of us to live alone."

"I think I would have liked your mother."

"And she," he said, brushing a finger along her arm, "would have liked you."

Esther looked up at him and for a moment, was once again snared by the sheer power of his physical presence. His hair was wind tousled. His cheekbones and nose were a deep red brown and his T-shirt clung to the broad stretch of his chest.

She turned back to the dishes, speaking to the sudsy water instead of the man in an effort to overcome the longing the sight of him created within her.

"I'm glad," she whispered, fighting herself once again. No matter how hard she tried, she couldn't stop wanting him. Her dreams at night paraded a thousand fantasies of him across her mind, leaving her hot and restless with morning, irritable and hungry and—

"I like you, too," he said quietly, and stepped up behind her. "This blouse drove me mad today."

She started when his hands fell onto her shoulders. "There's nothing seductive about this shirt, Alexander," she said to hide her nervousness. As if she didn't notice his thumbs drawing circles along her collarbone, she dropped a plastic cup into the drainer. "It even has long sleeves."

His hair brushed her ear an instant before his lips touched her neck. "You really have no idea, do you?"

"No idea?" she echoed weakly, closing her eyes as his tongue traced a spiral from the hollow below her ear to the edge of the blouse on her shoulder.

"How magnificent you are." His hands traveled down her arms and back up again. Against her back, his body radiated heat and strength. "You're so strong and vibrant and sexy."

"Peasant stock," she said, struggling for a lightly mocking tone. But the words came out on a breathy note.

"Mmm." The sound vibrated from his mouth into her body. He suckled her earlobe, nibbling gently. His beard grazed her shoulder. He caught the airy fabric of her skirt and edged it upward until his palm, warm and callused, fell against her bare thigh. She sucked in a breath. "Alexander."

"I've wanted to do this all day," he whispered. The voluminous fabric cloaked his hand, but his fingers traced erotic patterns over her thigh. "So strong and firm." His other hand dropped and burrowed beneath her skirt on the other side, so his wide broad palms with their rough calluses were simultaneously moving over both legs. "Your skin is as soft as a cloud," he murmured, pressing closer into her bottom until she felt his sudden and fierce arousal. Her hips weakened and she leaned into him, dangling her gloved hands in soapy dishwater.

With his nose, he nudged the hair away from her neck and planted kisses at her nape, his fingers under her skirt circling higher on her thigh. "You are incredible, Esther." He kissed her shoulder and neck and ear, his beard a tantalizing addition to each movement, the silky curls of his head brushing new fire into the cells of her cheek and ear and jaw.

Esther felt as if every atom of her body were being caressed simultaneously and she trembled. She heard a small, helpless sound and realized vaguely it had come from her throat. She found her head falling backward to rest against his shoulder as his tongue danced against the edge of her ear, teasing, and then he burned a trail over her jaw. At the same time, he lifted her skirt and wrapped his bare leg around hers beneath the fabric. She sagged against him, lost in a haze of Alexander's making.

"I want you, Esther," he breathed into her ear, and then his mouth was open on her shoulder, tugging with a gentle suckling at the tender flesh.

She tore off the gloves on her hands and turned in his embrace. With a groan, Alexander lifted his head to kiss her, his hands below her skirt skimming up the backs of her thighs until her bottom was cupped in his palms. He pressed himself into the aching juncture of her thighs.

Esther moaned softly and the sound seemed to inflame him. His fingers pushed below the fragile barrier of her panties, his tongue danced an exquisite ballet of passion over her lips, and his beard and the silky curls of his head brushed her flesh.

A building wave pushed through her and she clutched him to her, unable to breathe or think. He moved his hips gently against her and his strong, callused fingers spread in radiating circles below her skirt. She quivered with a rippling, aching desire and pushed against him, longing for a more complete joining—

She realized with an icy shock that she was much too close to losing control. With a tiny cry of dismay, she pulled her mouth from his, grabbing his arms.

"Stop, Alexander." Her voice was throaty and husky with need.

He released her instantly, but didn't move away. He threaded his hands into her hair, forcing her to look at him. With exquisite tenderness, he kissed her lips. His eyes glowed turquoise. "You're a magnificent woman, Esther. I want to make love to you the way you were meant to be loved."

She swallowed, mesmerized by his gaze and the sound of his British voice, gone hot and soft with passion.

He stepped away a little and gently smoothed her skirt, then pressed another small, hungry kiss to her mouth. "When you're ready, Esther, I will be waiting."

And then, he was gone.

Chapter Ten

As Esther sorted the children's clothing Wednesday night in preparation for their trip, Alexander's words still echoed in her mind.

She had concentrated as much as possible on her children through the days just past, aware that she would miss them desperately. Abe had enjoyed tending the store so much that she had asked him to take over all day today, and taken the boys swimming and then out for hamburgers.

Esther had seen Alexander only twice. Monday night at the dojo, he had been going through his exercise in a room off the main one and she had not disturbed him. Tuesday in class, he was calm and tender, even teasing, but he didn't make any effort to sway her toward him. It made her wonder if she had imagined the whole thing Sunday evening.

And then, toward the end of class, she looked up to find his eyes upon her, the color that electric turquoise, and she knew his thoughts. Her body tautened, glistened with swift hunger, but she hurried away after class, suddenly very afraid of him.

When you're ready, Esther, I will be waiting.

Her body was ready—had probably been ready the instant she'd seen his beautiful form working with such power and grace that day in the dojo. Bodies were like that, she thought with a smile, folding socks. They cared little for reason or emotion or even suitability of time and place. If hormone-driven bodies ruled the world, it would have disintegrated before it had had a chance to begin.

So she had to ignore the siren call of her body, the urgings of her loins to have done with it. She had to look at the emotional angle—both his and hers—and the logical ones.

Logic. She sighed. Not good. His ordered, balanced life-style was on a direct collision course with her haphazard style. He didn't realize it, but their worlds were very, very different. On the other hand, he was adaptable, or seemed to be. He never seemed to mind the children, not their noise or their bickering or their messes. In fact, he seemed to like looking at the world through their eyes.

She counted shorts and jeans and stacked a reasonable number of both into the suitcase. Okay, she thought, so the positive outweighed the negative in the logic column. Two pluses.

Emotion.

The biggie. Both hers and his. Every instinct she owned warned her that he had not come to terms with his emotional wounds. His late wife was still vague in

Esther's mind and that worried her. Did he still grieve the woman herself, or was it fear of loss that lingered in the abrupt shadows that could cloud his eyes? Esther didn't know.

He was undoubtedly infatuated with Esther. Perhaps he might even fall in love with her. It would be good for him if he did. Loving would heal him. She just didn't know if he would let her close enough to the true heart of him for that to happen.

And that was the real reason she hesitated to let their passion have its reign—once she made love with Alexander, her life would be altered forever. There would be no holding back. He would open and expose every single inch of her soul, and would do it so joyfully, carefully and intently that she would be unable to hide anything.

There was danger in her openness. It had taken her many years to realize it, years of aching at the closed limits of other people. In defense, she had learned to erect a screen with strangers and choose her friends with great care.

But once she allowed someone into her inner circle, she was unable to maintain her reserve. She had a great questing hunger to understand and love the people in her life; something within her flowed out to embrace and share all that was, all that could be.

If she made love with Alexander, the small walls of protection she had managed to keep in place against him would crumble. He needed that unadulterated giving, the flow of her against his wounded soul—it would ease and heal the torn places he barely knew existed.

But what would happen to her if he found that he couldn't risk loving her, after all?

It would be devastating—worse than leaving her degree unfinished, worse than learning her ex-husband was unfaithful, worse than the wrenching difficulty of her divorce.

Before she risked that irreversible leap, she needed to know more about him, his feelings, his wounds. Only then could she make a wise decision about whether or not to move forward.

In class on Thursday, the student presentations began. The enthusiastic and fanatical young man who had argued and poked an arrow of intellectual challenge through the fabric of every argument wanted to go first. The subject he'd chosen was hygiene. As Esther settled next to Alexander in order to listen to his lecture, Alexander leaned over. In a whisper, he said, "This will be interesting—I guarantee it."

And it was. One of the qualities that made Keith so appealing was that, unlike many of the others, he approached everything with a sense of humor. So his presentation was sparkling and light, in spite of the grim statistics he cited.

Finally he wrapped up. "The disposal—or lack of the same—of sewage in the dark ages makes most of us shudder. We've definitely come a long way toward eliminating the diseases caused by such carelessness—typhoid and cholera, that kind of thing." He nodded. "Yes, we dispose of our sewage and organic waste very properly now."

He smiled slightly. "But have we really become more civilized? Instead of fecal matter and rotting vegetables in our rivers, there's now radioactive waste and chemical poisons from factories. Instead of a ditch in the middle of the street running with the waste of bodies, our streets are littered with everything from fast-food wrappers to discarded needles. Even those of us who wouldn't think of dropping a candy wrapper on the street will generate a ton of trash every year—trash we have no way to properly dispose of."

Esther glanced at Alexander, and found that he was smiling at the youth. Keith caught the expression on his professor's face and flushed in pride, then gave a little mock bow.

The class applauded, and within minutes, a rousing debate was in progress. For Esther, it was exhilarating and challenging. Although she didn't participate, she followed the arguments carefully, weighing out both sides in her own mind for later sorting.

When the class time ended, Alexander gestured toward Keith, keeping him back after the others had left. "That was quite well done," Alexander said.

"Thanks, Dr. Stone."

"I'd like to talk to you about your plans following graduation, if you wouldn't mind. Are you free sometime tomorrow morning?"

"Sure. About ten?"

"Fine. You know where my office is."

"See you." He lifted a hand to both Esther and Alexander, then shouldered his heavy book bag and wandered out.

Alexander looked at her. "Will you join me for coffee this morning? I overslept and had no chance to eat breakfast."

"The orderly and disciplined Alexander Stone overslept?" Esther said with raised eyebrows. "What's the world coming to?"

He brushed her forearm with his index finger. "If my dreams of a certain lovely redhead didn't so torment me," he said quietly, "I'd likely be on time."

Esther said nothing. She lowered her eyes, feeling the sweep of yearning overtake her. "Let's go get some breakfast," she said finally.

Out on the university grounds, with warm summer sunshine streaming through the trees, the oddly claustrophobic sense of desire that had descended over Esther at his hint of dreams evaporated. She looked at him. "Keith is a natural teacher. Is that what you're going to discuss with him?"

"Partly. The trouble is, he's on scholarships and just recently wed. The last six months have been a struggle for him and another student told me this morning that his wife is going to have a baby."

Esther made a sympathetic noise.

"Yes," Alexander said. "In fact, your experiences are what triggered my decision to see if I might be able to help him."

A pang touched her—if only there had been someone willing to go to bat for her, how different things might be now. "I think that's wonderful," she said. "What are you going to do?"

"I wanted to talk to you about that." He took her hand and wrapped it around his elbow, covering it with his own hand. "What would have made it possible for you to continue with your studies? Was it money or time that made it impossible?"

Ruefully Esther said, "What I needed was a different husband." She sighed. "It was time, mainly, for me. John wanted me home with the children. But that also led to questions of money, because it was impossible to hold a job, do my studies and care for Daniel all at once.''

''Didn't he help you?''

Esther hesitated, knowing how cruel her answer would make John seem. ''No, Alexander, he was opposed to me leaving the children at all.'' Their walk had carried them to a small bridge over a pond and she paused there to look at Alexander. ''But it's a lot more complicated than it seems. He's not a bad person. His mother was an alcoholic and abused him.'' A flicker of sympathy showed on Alexander's craggy features, giving her courage to continue. ''He wanted the boys to have the mother he never did, and I guess I wanted to show him that they would.''

''You needn't defend him to me, Esther.''

She smiled. ''Maybe I'm defending him to me.''

''You're very hard on yourself,'' he said, inclining his head. ''We all make mistakes, you know. And you can hardly call the time you spent with John a mistake. You have your children, and since Jeremy will be in school next year, there's no reason you can't go ahead with your degree, as well.''

''Is that so?''

''Yes.'' He took her hand. ''But that's not what I meant to discuss this morning. I am starving.''

''What are you going to do for Keith?'' she asked.

''I'm not quite sure. Susan was quite wealthy—her father built a fortune in manufacturing—and she asked me to see that some of that money be used for this kind of thing.''

''Why not a scholarship or something?''

He shook his head. ''She felt that scholarships, no matter how well administered, often had too many conditions attached. So instead of setting it up to be given to graduate students in history or single parents or struggling sons of the working class—'' he lifted a brow sardonically ''—she asked me to keep my eyes open as long as I taught, and when I retired, to pass the baton to someone I felt would do it well.''

They had reached the door of the café, and Esther paused, touched. ''What a kind person she must have been.''

''Yes.'' But instead of a sad light that sometimes clouded his eyes, this time the kaleidoscope irises twinkled. ''But no saint, I assure you.''

She smiled and stepped inside as he held the door. But in light of the resolve she had made the night before, the opportunity was too good to pass up. As a young waitress poured fragrant coffee into heavy mugs, Esther asked, ''What was she like, Alexander?''

''Who?'' He seemed genuinely bewildered. ''Oh, Susan?'' He paused to tell the waitress to bring him an omelet.

''Just coffee for me,'' Esther said.

He looked out the window for a moment, then finally looked at Esther, a fond expression gentling the harsh planes of his face. ''She was silly,'' he said. ''She liked practical jokes and magic tricks and could tell a filthy story and get away with it because she looked like a nun.''

''Was she pretty?''

The twinkle returned to his eyes. ''I believe you're a bit jealous.''

''Maybe a little,'' Esther admitted. ''Maybe curious is a better word.''

He stirred cream into his coffee. ''Well, Susan was many things—smart and funny and terribly clever, but no, she wasn't particularly pretty. She was always too thin and a bit frail in spite of her vitality." He tugged his beard. "But she had enormous gray eyes that were quite beautiful, and you forgot after a while that there were any prettier women because she had such presence."

A nudge of something half remembered flickered in Esther's mind, but she ignored it. Clasping her hands tightly in front of her, she leaned over the table. "Are you still in love with her, Alexander?"

For a long moment, he didn't answer. In that moment, Esther saw all the things about him that she had grown so fond of—all the physical details that made him different from every other male on the planet. She let her gaze touch each detail: the hints of silver glittering through his dark curls, the swell of his lower lip against a frame of silky face hair, the breadth of his shoulders beneath his hand-tailored shirt, his beautiful long-fingered hands. Then she looked into his eyes for the answer she had to have, even if it meant she could no longer sit with him in the quiet of a weekday morning, drinking coffee at a window booth with students walking by.

"I will always love the memory of her, Esther," he said at last. "I spent fourteen years of my life with her, and you don't forget someone like that." He smiled and the twinkle shone like tiny stars through the sudden turquoise of his eyes. "But it's you that I think of in the dark of the night, that I dream of, that I want."

She blushed, because it suddenly seemed as if she'd been fishing for compliments.

As if he knew the conversation had made her shy, he sipped his coffee and looked out the window. "Esther," he said and frowned.

"What?" she asked, puzzled.

"If you had the resources, would you finish your degree?"

Esther bit her lip. Even the thought of it was terrifying. She wasn't sure she *could* do it. "I don't know," she said at last. It seemed as if she should add more to that, somehow, that she should articulate her reasons for not knowing, but how could she? She wasn't even sure what they were herself. "I haven't even let myself think about it since I left school."

The waitress brought his omelet and refilled their coffee cups. Alexander said nothing for several minutes. Finally he looked at her with a serious expression in his eyes. "You're a natural healer, Esther. I hope you won't defer your dream much longer."

"Thank you."

He ate with relish and Esther watched him spreading jam on toast liberally. "I keep meaning to buy some of your rose-petal jelly," he commented.

"I've got to make a fresh batch this afternoon. A woman brought a bag of rose petals in this morning to trade for a gallon of lemonade." The thought didn't give her much pleasure. The day was going to be a hot one and she would much rather have spent the time with the children. But if she left them, the petals would be no good. "Hmm," she said, thinking aloud. "I wonder if I could make a decoction of the petals and wait until this weekend to make the jelly."

"Try it," he commented. "And if it works, may I come over and learn your secret recipe?"

She laughed, then inclined her head. "There's an elaborate initiation and incantation, but I suppose I can share it with you."

The small radiating lines around his eyes creased with humor. "Perhaps I ought to dust off the robe I keep around for such sacred occasions." He finished his breakfast with a sigh of satisfaction and lifted his coffee. "When are the boys leaving?"

"John is coming to get them at nine in the morning." She looked at her watch. "Which means I'd better get back and finish the packing."

"All right. I'm going to sit here a while longer."

She smiled. "Ponder the unponderables?"

"Something like that." He stood up with her. "Call me if you need anything, will you?"

"I will. Thanks."

Esther cooked all the children's favorite foods for supper, hot dogs and macaroni and cheese, strawberry-banana gelatin with bananas, and German chocolate cake. Afterward, they went through their lists carefully, making sure nothing had been forgotten. Each had several favorite toys, plenty of clothes, jackets and sweaters and sturdy shoes. She gave them baths and washed their hair, then clipped their fingernails and toenails, which they loved for some reason Esther had never been able to fathom.

"Okay, guys. Each of you pick a book and I'll read to you, then you need to get to sleep."

Jeremy chose his copy of *Owl Moon,* which told the story of a little girl and her father going owling in the middle of a still winter night. She ruffled his silky curls as he put it in her lap. "I remember when I checked this book out of the library the first time," she said with a smile. "You loved it so much that we renewed it three times."

"Yep, but this one's mine," he said.

"Yes." She'd given it to him for his birthday and nearly teared up over his excitement at opening the present—he'd literally shrieked with joy.

Daniel gave her his hand-me-down copy of Uncle Wiggly stories. "Can we read three?"

She patted the spot next to her on the bed. "I'll read five."

"All right!" He snuggled next to her.

Surrounded by the moist warmth of them, Esther read. She absorbed the soap-fresh smell of their skin, the herbal scent of the shampoo, admired the rosy glow of scrubbed little-boy faces. Although sometimes she hurried through bedtime stories because there were a dozen chores she had to do before she could go to bed herself, tonight she was sorry when it was time for them to climb into their bunk beds.

She tucked them in, feeling a dragging sense of unease, one that had bothered her all day. She didn't believe in premonitions, but thought there might have been something she'd overlooked. As she listened to their prayers, she tried to think what it could be, but nothing jelled.

Squatting down to hug Jeremy, she said, "You remember, now, horses are very strong animals and you have to be very careful with them."

"I know," he said with a note of impatience.

"Okay." She smiled and rose to hug Daniel on the top bunk. "You know you can call me whenever you want to."

Tears flooded his brilliant eyes. "If I don't like it there, can I come home?"

Esther swallowed back the flood of emotion that threatened to overwhelm her. "Of course you can. But

I think you'll have a wonderful time. Your daddy is so excited.''

He hugged her hard. ''I wish you could come, too.''

''I know.'' She kissed his forehead. ''Go to sleep now. I'll see you in the morning.''

As she went downstairs, the strange sense of doom stuck with her. What had she forgotten?

She called Melissa, then Abe, and got no answer. She considered calling Alexander, but felt too dangerously weepy and tired to burden him. Finally she called her mother in Georgia. The soft tones of the thick Southern voice comforted her as nothing else could have. Even her father, as brisk and uncomfortable as always with displays of affection, made her feel better.

As she hung up, she was yawning. It had been a long week. What she needed was a good night's sleep.

But she didn't get it. She dreamed of John driving away in the car with the children while she chased behind it, holding up something she couldn't identify that he'd forgotten to take with him. When she looked down to see what it was, she found she held a safe in her hands—a safe to which only Esther knew the combination.

Finally, hot and thirsty, she got up just before dawn and went downstairs for a cup of coffee. She took it out into the backyard, wearing a sweater against the morning chill. A blackbird sang in an elm tree and a flutter of wrens chirped in the herb garden, catching bugs for breakfast. In the east, a pale glow heralded the rising sun.

The imagery of her dream wasn't hard to fathom. Despite all her protests to the contrary, she was worried that John would be unable to keep the children safe from harm. That was what had worried her last night. It was silly. If anything, he was overprotective.

The calm quiet of nature at dawn eased her worry and she went back inside to make a grocery list. She flicked on the dining room light, and the bulb, with a buzz and a pop, burned out. Rolling her eyes, she went to the kitchen for a fresh bulb.

Befuddled by the restless night, she forgot what she'd come for and stood in the middle of the room, trying to remember. She noticed the coleus drooping in the window and gave it a drink, then absently plucked off a few withered leaves.

Light bulb. She snapped her fingers, fished one from the cupboard and returned to the dining room.

An unmistakable odor of fire greeted her. In horror, she glanced up to see a tendril of smoke curling from the nail holes around the light fixture.

She raced upstairs to the boys' room, flinging back their covers. "Get up," she said in an urgent voice. "Get up!" She shook Jeremy and then Daniel, who barely stirred. Jeremy sat up blinking. "Get out of bed and go outside right now," she told her youngest, and stood up to scoop the sleeping Daniel into her arms.

He flopped on her shoulder, all fifty pounds of him, but she didn't dare take the time she'd need to get him awake enough to walk on his own.

"Why, Mommy?" Jeremy asked. He padded behind her down the stairs. "Why?"

"Let's just get outside, okay?"

"But I don't have my shoes!"

"You can go out without them, honey. Just this once, it'll be okay." Breathing hard over the strain of carrying Daniel down the long, steep stairs, she urged Jeremy along. "Don't worry. Let's just get outside."

Smoke was filling the dining room by the time they reached the bottom of the steps and her heart squeezed painfully.

Jeremy stopped. "A fire! Mommy!"

"I know, Jeremy. Come *on!*"

Once all three of them were safely out in the front yard, Esther ran next door to use the telephone. The sun was beginning to peek over the horizon as she pounded frantically at the heavy wooden door. "Mr. Hernandez! Help!" she cried, and was about to jump down from the porch and try another neighbor when the elderly man flung open the door.

Before he could speak, she said, "Oh, thank God. My house is on fire. Call the fire department, please."

He whirled, instantly awake, and leaving the door open, ran toward his kitchen. Trusting in his lightning response, she returned to her boys, who were both, by now, crying.

She gathered them into her arms. "Shh. The fire department is coming. It'll be okay." But over their heads she saw black smoke drifting lazily out an open window. The house was eighty years old—heaven only knew what had gathered between the walls.

Suddenly Jeremy broke away from her. "My blanket!" he screeched, running for the house. "My blanket's on my bed!"

"No!" Esther cried, and tackled him as he reached the steps. "No, Jeremy. I'm sorry. You can't go in there." She carried him back to the distant spot by the sidewalks as he burst into tears. "It'll be okay, honey. The firemen will be here and put out the fire."

Mr. Hernandez, wrapped in a striped bathrobe, hurried out. "They're on their way." He glanced at the window and saw the smoke. "I hope they hurry," he said grimly, then looked at the shivering children. "What am I thinking?" he muttered. "You boys come in my house and have hot chocolate, eh? We'll watch the firemen through the windows."

A scream of sirens sounded in the distance. "He's right, boys. Go on inside with Mr. Hernandez and as soon as I talk to the firemen, I'll be in, too."

Even summer mornings were chilly so close to the mountains and the boys, dressed only in lightweight pajamas, agreed. Esther tugged her sweater more closely around her demure cotton nightgown, thankful she had been up so early, that this had happened in the daytime....

She shuddered as the fire truck came into view, pushing away all thoughts of "what if?" There was enough to deal with as it was.

In the end, it didn't take long to get the fire under control. It had traveled through the ceiling in the dining room, into the wall between the two bedrooms upstairs. When it was put out, and the firemen had gathered up most of their tools and hoses, a strapping fireman walked over to Esther. "You know how the fire started, ma'am?"

"Not exactly," she replied. "But I can guess. The wiring?"

He made a grim face. "Yeah." He tipped his hat back on his head and met her eyes. "I got a look at it behind that wall, and I'm afraid I'm going to have to recommend to the chief that this be declared unsafe to occupy until you get that rewired."

Esther took a long breath and blew it out, looking at the house. She nodded. "I understand."

"You were real lucky," he commented.

"I know," she said, but her mind was filling with the whirl of problems the decree would cause. She had no idea how much it would cost to do the rewiring and in the meantime, she had no place to stay or any means of supporting herself. "Thank you," she said.

"I shut the electricity off in the back there." He seemed to notice her bare feet for the first time. "You can get some of your stuff after we get the cleanup done, but in the meantime, you want one of us to get you and your boys some clothes?"

Still stunned, Esther just looked at him for a moment. "Uh, there's a suitcase in my kitchen."

He nodded.

Then she remembered Jeremy hurtling toward the house. "There is something you could get for me, if you would." She felt numb. "In the back bedroom, there's a small blue quilt. Maybe on the top bunk."

He pursed his lips briefly, seemed about to say something, then said, "I'll go look."

The fireman returned a few minutes later, carrying the suitcase she had packed for the children as well as the sooty, soggy blanket. "This it?" he asked and smiled.

She breathed a sigh of relief. "Yes."

"It fell on the floor," he commented, handing it over. "Good thing." He cleared his throat. "The mattresses were right up against that wall. They got eaten up a little. Have to replace them."

Again, Esther nodded dumbly. There was no sensation at all within her. Nothing. She carried the suitcase and blanket over to Mr. Hernandez's house, got the boys dressed, rinsed the smoky blanket in the sink and hung it over his porch railing to dry. A bevy of neighbors brought food and coffee. Someone gave

Esther a housedress to wear, although she was still barefoot.

She called John and he came over in a matter of minutes. "Are you guys okay?" he asked with concern.

"Daddy!" Jeremy screeched. "My blanket got all dirty with smoke!"

"It did?" he said, then stood up and touched Esther's arm. "I'm sorry, Esther."

"Why?"

"I should have realized you had a short up there and that's why you had to put in a new light bulb so often. Damn." Hands on his hips, he stared at the house. "I'll understand if you want to cancel the trip to the ranch."

Daniel overheard and jumped to his feet. "No! Please, Mommy?"

Esther shook her head. "No. Considering everything, this is best. By the time they come back, I'll have worked this out somehow."

"Are you sure? You look a little shaky."

"I *am* a little shaky," she admitted. "But really, taking them to the ranch is the best possible solution."

He scowled. "Okay," he said finally and picked up the suitcase. "You call if you want me to bring them back, or if you want to come up to the ranch or anything, okay?"

At moments like this, when John let his good heart show, she remembered why she had loved him once. "I will," she said with a smile. "Take good care of them, John," she said.

"Count on it, kid." He chucked her on the chin lightly.

She smiled halfheartedly and walked outside with him. She felt as brittle as old glass as she picked up Jeremy's blanket, but in a way, the fire had relieved her odd sense of impending disaster. Her subconscious had obviously been picking up the same warnings John had cursed over—she shouldn't have had to replace light bulbs so frequently.

"Esther!"

She looked up, still lost in her shaky daze, and walking toward them was Alexander. Sunlight glinted in his dark curls and he walked with the long strides and easy grace she had grown accustomed to.

And quite suddenly her numbness faded, to be replaced with an almost overwhelming sense of relief. He took one look at her face and pulled her close without a word. Esther let go of a long, shaky breath, pressing her face into the comfort of his powerful chest, smelling soap and cologne and the heady notes of the man himself.

"Alexander," she said quietly. Thank God.

Chapter Eleven

Alexander took her to his house when the children had departed. He showed her to the bathroom and brought out fresh towels. Then, since she had no shoes and only the baggy blue housedress a neighbor had loaned her to wear, he drove to a nearby department store and purchased a pair of sandals and a simple sleeveless dress he thought looked right for her. He even bought panties, but floundered when he came to a bra. Frowning, he asked a salesclerk for advice and she brought him a sort of generic, stretchy garment she assured him would work.

When he returned to his house, Esther sat on the front porch, a cup of coffee on the boards beside her. Her hair, still damp, floated in glittering waves around her porcelain face. She saw Alexander and pressed a finger to her ripe lips, a shine of amusement in her eyes. Puzzled, he paused—and his mouth nearly dropped.

For there below a juniper bush was Piwacket, chasing a long piece of string Esther wiggled between the branches. The cat's eyes were wide and bright, his enormous paws batting the string as playfully as if he were a kitten.

He grinned. "Tame all sorts of wild beasts, don't you?" he said dryly.

Piwacket looked up at the sound of Alexander's voice and sauntered out into the yard, ignoring Esther completely.

She chuckled, the sound as rich as good cognac. "I guess I'm only allowed his attention if you're not around." She lifted one side of her mouth in a wry smile. "Image is everything."

"When image is all you've got, I suppose it is." He handed her the bag he carried. "I picked up a few things for you. While you change, I'll fix some breakfast."

Esther peeked into the bag and a soft rosy color stained her cheeks. "You thought of everything."

He laughed softly at the surprise in her tone. "I hope you don't mind the liberty, but I thought you'd want to get moving as soon as possible."

She stood up and the baggy blue housedress billowed out around her. As if noticing it for the first time, she looked down, then up to Alexander. "It was thoughtful of you. Thanks." The smile faded, and in her deep brown eyes flickered another emotion—something warm and hungry. She touched his beard with her fingers. "I was so glad to see you this morning. Why did you come?"

"I thought you might like the company, since your children were leaving."

She cocked her head, smiling gently, her pale red hair caressing one cheek. Then she bent from her spot on the step above him and kissed his mouth. "Thank you."

He touched her jaw. "You're quite welcome."

When she returned to the kitchen a few minutes later, he had just poured the batter for a waffle into the iron, and a skillet full of bacon sizzled on the stove. "Everything fit all right?"

"Just fine." She whirled, the skirt of the green dress flaring up around her legs. "This is pretty," she said with a grin, and touched her chest above the scoop neck. "But I can tell a man picked it out."

"It looks good on you," he returned unapologetically, frankly admiring the modest but enticing swell of white breasts, the dip of her waist, the rounded flesh of her arms. He was pleased to have judged her size so accurately.

"Thanks." She lifted a wry eyebrow. "I can't believe you got my shoes right."

"You know, I almost bought a size or two smaller, and I remembered Abe teasing you about your gunboats."

She burst out laughing. "Well, ''d love to protest demurely, but you see they're honestly a size ten. Perfect fit." She settled at the table. "Can I do anything?"

"Not at all. I called the school and canceled my classes. Perhaps you ought to make a list of what needs to be done today."

"I already did." She tapped her head. "It's right here. I've got to hire someone to clean up and repair the damage, and get the perishables out of the cooler in the store." She sighed. "And although it probably can't get done today, I have to get estimates on the wiring."

"Let me put out some feelers among the faculty." He pulled bacon from the fat to drain on paper towels. "I seem to remember several people talking about a handyman who does almost everything. They all use him."

"Great."

He paused, weighing his next words carefully. "Esther, have you given any thought to where you'll stay?"

"I really haven't gotten that far."

"Will you stay here?" He met her eyes directly, neither leering nor promising celibacy. He wouldn't lie and tell her it was only because he was concerned about her—although that was certainly part of it. But he wanted her here under his roof for himself, as well.

And she met his eyes honestly, offering no false protestations of modesty, nor asking for promises. She glanced at her hands, once, then back to his face. "I'd like that," she said softly.

For an instant, the room was filled with the unspoken agreement below their words. The last barriers had been dropped. A magnetic energy sizzled between them, glowed fiercely, then faded back to embers as Alexander calmly smiled. "Good."

The day was spent estimating and cleaning up. Esther found, to her relief, that the damage was not nearly as terrible as her mind had been conjuring it to be. The ceiling in the dining room was charred and unsafe, and a layer of soot coated almost everything in the rooms adjoining the dining room downstairs. Thanks to a privacy door between the living quarters and the store, none of the merchandise had been damaged.

Upstairs was the worst of it. At the sight of the boys' mattresses, charred and half-eaten by the fire that had raged up the wall next to them, she felt nauseous. Everything was soggy—all their toys, the rug, their bedding. It would all have to be replaced. She bent over the bookcase, fearing the worst. Some of the books were rippling with the effect of water, their covers buckling.

But in typical sloppiness, Esther had not replaced the books she had read to the children the night before. Instead, she had stacked them atop a metal dresser in the corner. She grinned, picking them up. The dustcover of *Owl Moon* was dotted with water, but other than that, both books were intact. She hugged them to her chest.

Her own room stunk with smoke, but nothing had been damaged—at least she didn't think so until she opened the closet to get her clothes. But here, the fire had played the same game as with the boys' mattresses—her clothes were chewed and scorched by fire. Anything unburned was sodden and smelled horrible.

But again, her careless habits were a boon. On a chair near her bed were several favorite skirts and blouses. She'd taken them out yesterday with the intent of ironing them, and when she ran behind, never got around to putting them away. Her favorite Indian cotton was there, and her yellow blouse. She picked them up, hugging them as she'd hugged the books. Thank God for small favors.

By evening, she was exhausted and touchy. Alexander, with typical sensitivity, seemed to sense her mood and after supper left her alone while he went to the dojo.

After he left, she wandered into the backyard. Unlike her own garden, full of overgrown tomato plants and unruly herbs, his beds were neatly laid out, the colors and heights of the flowers meshing in meticulously planned order. She trailed through thick, emerald grass along the edges of the garden, pausing here and there to admire a rose or lily. He had an extravagant collection of tiger lilies that were bursting now into full bloom—and she would have bet quite a sum of money that it had been Susan's idea to plant them. She could see Alexander taking pride in his beautiful roses, which were a difficult flower to grow well, but the tiger lilies were frivolous, ruffly blossoms in shades of peach and white and pink. Somehow, she couldn't imagine the lion man bothering with them.

Toward the back fence was a small wood-and-iron bench. Esther settled there, looking back over the yard to the house. The order of the flower beds somehow gave her a feeling of serenity she would never have expected. She thought she preferred gardens, like life, to be a little disorderly.

But as she eyed the weeded rows between soft blue ageratums and a healthy stand of marigolds behind, she wished faintly that she had enough foresight to plant a garden that looked like that. Blue and small, yellow and bushy, red and tall. There was nothing even faintly compulsive about his neatness—the water hoses were coiled in a haphazard heap near the faucet, and a collection of rakes and other long-handled tools leaned negligently against a tree.

Serene. The gardens were serene—a calm place to which you could retreat from the tangle of life. Here, there was order, beauty, calm.

Had Susan sat here, once upon a time? Esther looked toward the house, expecting with half her mind to see a transparent face at the window—a presence protesting Esther. Instead, a curtain pulled out by a breeze flapped against the painted brick wall. If anything, there was a sense of benevolence here, an odd sense of welcome and sympathy.

"Do you mind?" Esther said aloud softly. Her sense of reality was so distorted by the long, long day that she didn't even think it was odd to be speaking aloud to no one. She looked at the sky, and back to the window with its lace curtain and thought of the ceramic pitcher in the front window that had always struck her with its sense of peace.

"Do you mind?" she asked again, and now she knew she was not speaking to no one, but to Susan, who had once admired the tiger lilies, had once sat on this bench, her ankles tickled by long strands of uncut grass.

"I'll mind." Her eyes filled with tears. "Not because I'm afraid, but because of all the things I'll miss." She took a breath, unable to stem the rising emotion. "I'll miss my children, even if they're grown up men by then. I'll miss flowers and coffee and morning rainstorms. It's all so incredible and it goes so fast—and you just never know what will happen, do you?"

She closed her eyes and just let the tears roll over her face, tears of release and joy and sorrow. She listened to birds chirping and the last whirring of insects before twilight closed in. She smelled roses and wet

grass, felt the cool mountain air on her arms and the
gentle clasp of leather sandals upon her feet.

Then, cutting through everything else, was the scent
of Alexander. She opened her eyes to find him standing silently before her, the mane of dark hair tumbling around his face. An expression of such soft
passion lit his features that she nearly wept again for
the tenderness she saw.

As he reached down to take her hand gently in his
own, drawing her into his arms, Esther felt her heart
expand until it seemed it would burst her chest.

*Do you mind, Susan, that I've fallen in love with
him?*

She wrapped her arms around him, feeling an ache
as he brushed the wet from her cheeks with his fingers, and thought she heard a sweet answer ringing
through her. *Love him,* it whispered. *Love him.*

''Esther,'' he breathed, pressing her head into the
hollow of his shoulder. He held her tight and rocked
her in an ancient gesture of comfort. They stood there
swaying for a long time in the pale lavender gloam-
ing. Esther rested against him and closed her eyes, as
messages, too deep and primal for words, passed between their bodies, between their cells, between their
souls.

When Esther lifted her head, he looked at her a long
moment. There in his changeable eyes she saw the
turquoise of his passion mixed with the gray of his
long loneliness, and something as expectant as the
emotion she felt now in her heart.

He kissed her. A slow, gentle kiss, one of supplica-
tion and healing, of hunger and tenderness. His lips
told her he knew this moment was not one to be undertaken lightly. It was the velveteen runner spread

below the chalice and gold plate at church; it was a pledge of honor.

Esther returned it, holding his face against her palm, feeling the tiny movements of his jaw below the silkiness of his beard. She answered his gentle question with a promise of her own—she knew the night would change her. And she was ready.

He led her through the quiet yard and upstairs into his broad bedroom. There he paused, holding her hand. "Do you mind being here?" he asked softly.

"No." She reached for the buttons on her dress, but he covered her hands with his own, stepping close.

The room was filled with pearl-gray light as she dropped her hands to her side. A hush of waiting fell and Esther looked into Alexander's face. He loosened her buttons one by one in his unhurried way, his fingers skimming the exposed few inches of flesh each time a button freed more of her. When the dress was open to the waist, he bent his glossy head to kiss the hollow between her breasts, his touch as light as the dying sounds of day beyond the window.

And when he lifted his head once more, Esther let her eyes wash over the newly beloved face in wonder, her gaze touching his strong, high brow and the blunt nose, his full lower lip and the powerful line of his jaw below the silvered beard.

Her dress, then her undergarments fell away, leaving her naked before him. Alexander ran reverent hands over her shoulders, down her arms, over her breasts and rib cage and belly. "You are beautiful beyond words, Esther," he murmured, his hands lightly stroking her waist. He bent his head to kiss her shoulder, his hands cupping her breasts, and she heard his breath stir raggedly in his throat, a rough sound of wonder, of hunger, of pain and joy.

Her legs quivered and a slow fire of awakening began to burn through her body. She grasped his head in her hands, feeling the curls spring up to embrace her fingers. His clothing rasped against her naked body, and Esther stepped back.

She unbuttoned his shirt, smiling at him. "What's good for the goose," she whispered, pushing the fabric from his lean, muscled torso, "is good for the gander." She leaned forward and took a flat nipple into her mouth, her hands working with the buttons on his trousers. She was careless with her hands, letting them brush the rigid heat of his erection below the cloth as if by accident. She laughed low in her throat when he growled softly, his fingers digging into her shoulders.

Then he, too, stood naked in the still room. Esther felt a physical pain pass through her at the splendor of his body—his broad shoulders and tapering torso and leanly muscular hips. She opened her palms on the crisp hair of his chest, feeling supple skin and firm muscles below her fingers. She touched the rise of his biceps and his forearms and let her hands roam the outer curve of his thighs.

She wanted to tell him that he looked like a lion with his wild mane of curls and his tawny flesh. She wanted to tell him that she had never felt such a longing for the touch of anyone in her life as she longed for his now. Instead she swayed forward into his kiss, feeling his arms slip around her back, his naked chest touch her breasts, his bare stomach press into her own. He took her head almost savagely into his hand as he clasped her hard into him. She fell against him, tipping her head back into his palm and opening her mouth for the forceful thrust of his tongue.

She let herself be propelled toward the bed, where he laid her down gently. For a long, silent moment, he towered above her, his eyes washing over her body with unmistakable heat. He knelt beside her and with his hands touched the swell of her breasts and the belly she thought too fat, and thighs too strong and big to be feminine. Under the approval of his hands and eyes, Esther felt herself grow beautiful, delectable. She opened her arms and beckoned him.

And then he was with her, covering her with his hands and mouth, running his hair-furred leg over her smooth one, his hand over her rounded belly, his tongue over her lips.

A wild, primitive hunger beat a steady thrumming in Esther's veins and she found herself nearly biting his shoulder, his neck, his ear; she curled her leg around his and pressed herself upward.

Alexander grasped her shoulders. "It will be worth the wait," he whispered, pressing his lips to her forehead gently as his hands massaged the tight muscles of her neck. The edge of panic she felt began to ease away and a completely new sensation spread from the point between her eyebrows where his lips rested, radiating outward into her muscles. It was a warm tingle, a balm to the frantic ache. She still felt the press of his arousal against her belly, and the hunger to open to him did not ease, but the odd tingling freed her to explore him more slowly, and be explored in return.

He kissed her eyelids and her cheek and her jaw, moving without hurry. At the hollow of her throat, he paused, brushing it first with the hair of his beard, then his lips, and finally with his tongue. Esther let her hands run over the silk of his back, felt his hair brush her chin.

And still the hunger snaked through her limbs and cells and nerves, but it became like a dance—thrumming here, jumping wildly there.

As he moved to her breasts, he followed the same slow pattern, his beard grazing one gloriously sensitized tip, then the other. His lips touched the swelling flesh, following the curves one way now, another direction this time, and still Esther floated.

But when his mouth opened, wet and hot, to close over her nipple, she cried out with the sudden frenzy of dancing in her cells. He suckled there firmly, then flickered over her with his tongue, teasing and tugging with his lips until she writhed against him, lost.

His hand crept down her belly and spread her legs, his mouth still teasing her breasts. Esther went rigid for a moment, but he shifted to kiss her mouth just then, sliding his tongue between her lips as his hand slid exquisitely between her legs.

"Alexander," she said in a voice she barely recognized as her own. "Please."

And still his fingers toyed with her, creating a slow, building pressure. She reached for him in hunger and a desperate need to give pleasure even as she received it. She restlessly caressed his hips and thighs and back, then let her fingers graze his erection lightly. He groaned against her mouth and she dropped her fingertips lower still, to that soft, most vulnerable place on him.

With a powerful movement, he shifted over her. There, braced on steel arms, he looked down. His eyes glowed a vivid turquoise and his hair tumbled in wild disarray from the raking of her fingers and Esther realized her vision of him had come true—it was the lion who braced himself at her opening. His eyes locked on hers for a long, sober instant, and then he moved and they were joined.

Now there was no play. The sacrament was ready, and they partook. Alexander moved with fury and hunger and love. Esther met him with healing and passion and hope. In the growing darkness of the coming night, they moved together toward a pinnacle from which there would be no retreat or return. As they climbed and met the peak, Esther felt her heart knit with his, felt her soul and his mingle until there was no beginning of one or end to the other. As they tumbled from the pinnacle into the other side of their lives, they were one.

It was holy and perfect and shattering.

Cradled within her, shaken by the power of the moments just past, Alexander raised his head and cupped Esther's face between his hands. Her heavy-lidded eyes opened. He kissed her, tasting her ripe pink lips and the satin of her tongue. "I love to kiss you," he whispered and tasted her mouth again. He pushed his fingers through the soft cloud of hair tangled on the pillow. "And touch you."

Below him, her body was pliant and giving. He lifted himself a little and stroked her breast. He felt her tighten around him, felt his own body respond instantly. "Ah, Esther," he said, kissing her again and again. "You're a goddess, a queen."

She smiled and lifted her arms to wrap them around his neck, her fingers crawling into his hair. "And you are my king." A bubble of soft laughter rose in her throat and the sexy somnolence flooded her eyes.

"With kingly arms and kingly lips and a kingly—" she lifted her eyebrow wickedly "—sword."

"You like that, do you?" he replied, moving against her.

Her eyes drifted closed. "Mmm."

Without breaking the contact between them, he rolled over, taking her with him until she sat astride him, her hair tumbling around her face. Her white shoulders glowed with reflected light and her breath came in shallow, quick bits. He lifted his hands and spread his fingers open over her breasts, feeling an ache rise hard again at the sight of his dark fingers splaying over her pale flesh. She arched and the motion thrust the aroused tips of her breasts into his palms. Roughly he pulled her close, and sucked the tempting flesh into his mouth, rolling it over his tongue until she cried his name.

Amazed he could still be so unsatisfied, he pushed her backward and this time took her with a frenzy that had been lacking a moment before. She met his thrusts with arches and cries, tangling with him violently. The passion built again fervently, wildly, and he felt the fury edging through him and the quivering of Esther around him just as he felt their bodies slip a little. She cried out, throwing her arms and legs tightly around him as they slid on the discarded quilt to the floor. As they landed in a tangle of blankets and limbs, the explosions rocketed through them once again.

After a moment, Esther laughed throatily, shifting to pull a convenient blanket over their bodies as a chill crept through the room. He lay on his back and she rested her chin on his chest. With one finger, she reached up to trace a line through his beard. Her dark eyes were luminous and her cheeks had a healthy glow. "I've never fallen off a bed before," she said softly.

"Me, either," he said at last. He lifted her hand and kissed the palm. "But there's never been a woman who made me feel like you do."

Her gaze flickered away and he caught her chin. She looked at him, an oddly vulnerable expression in her eyes. "I've been dead, Esther. You've given me life again."

"You weren't dead," she whispered. "You were only asleep." She slid along his body until she could press kisses on his face. The soft press of her thighs and belly and breast against him sent echoes and prelude through his nerves. "It was my good luck to be the one to kiss you awake."

"No," he said, pulling up until he could look into the beautiful face. He kissed her solemnly, feeling a new emotion rise within him. "It was mine," he said with gravity. Before he could speak his love aloud he pressed his mouth to hers again, hearing her whispered words mirror the ones in his heart.

"I love you," she whispered. "I love you."

Chapter Twelve

Monday morning, Esther awakened alone for the first time since Friday evening. As she turned in the big bed, she felt her muscles protest weakly and she smiled softly in remembrance of all the delightful ways those muscles had been exercised.

She and Alexander had left the cocoon of his bed only for food and once for a shared shower. The rest of the time they had spent tangled together, loving and talking and laughing.

But now it was Monday morning. She snuggled under the covers for a few minutes more, admiring the soft light pushing at the shades on the east side of the room, wishing there were more days to spend with only Alexander, alone here with nothing to intrude. She wished for a sailboat awash on the Pacific for long weeks, the larder stocked with all they could possibly want. She wished for a deserted island or a cabin deep in a primitive forest.

Unfortunately he had classes to teach. She had a house that needed attention and a business that would go under if she didn't get someone in to make the repairs. Guiltily she realized she had not called Abe to tell him what had happened; if he'd come by the house over the weekend, he would be worried sick by now.

This thought finally propelled her out of bed and into the shower. She dressed and wandered out of Alexander's room in search of him. A door stood ajar down the hall and she paused to peek in.

It stretched the width of the house. Toward the front was the window with the ceramic pitcher and washbowl in front of it—her serenity room, Esther realized with a smile.

She laughed at the actual picture, because boxes were stacked on one wall, and the accumulations of several years sat on tables and in chairs. It wasn't sloppy—just disorganized.

Esther pushed the door open and went in, looking around in delight. Beyond the clutter, she saw that it fulfilled the promise she had imagined. Gentle light would fill the room at all times of day except early morning. A dusty sewing machine sat in one corner, and a dressmaker's dummy draped with a piece of cloth stood mutely alongside. The walls were painted a warm peach, and a wide border of green leaves traveled along a chair rail.

This had been Susan's place. The rest of the house, over the course of years since her death, had gradually taken on the stamp of Alexander's personality. Here, she lingered.

A small noise from the backyard drew Esther's attention and she wandered to the back windows. Below, in the dew-wet grass, was Alexander. Dressed only in his loose cotton trousers in spite of the chilly morning air, he performed his tai chi exercise. Pale sunlight danced in his dark curls and glistened over his naked, beautiful torso.

Esther touched her stomach, feeling it tighten, struck again by the power and grace he displayed. No movement was wasted, not a single stumble marred his smooth, circular gestures.

In some way, seeing him at work on his discipline underlined the mystery of him, the depth of his complicated personality. He was a history professor with a passion for intellectual challenge—who junked out on old movies and suspense novels. He was a neat widower who wore hand-tailored shirts and spoke in precise British syllables, and a man who could tumble with two young boys until they were gasping for breath. His eyes could twinkle as quickly as they could go that strange, bleak gray. He was a magnificent lover, powerful and tender, and a man who was desperately afraid to love again for fear he could not survive the loss it might entail.

And when he danced like this in the still morning, she saw he was a mystic who desperately needed to believe in something.

She turned away, leaving him to his privacy. Her hip bumped a pile of papers on the sewing table, sending them scattering to the floor. She bent to pick them up. As she reached for them, though, her hands froze on a photograph.

Esther picked it up, feeling a flutter of sorrow and memory—a memory that had tugged her when Alexander had told her of Susan's eyes.

The woman in the photograph was not pretty, but her eyes were as wide as a mountain sky, their color the shade of storm clouds. She laughed in the photo, showing good white teeth and powerful humor.

Esther had known her.

She settled on her knees, holding the picture in her hands, remembering. Before Esther had opened the organic foods store in the front of her house, she had worked in an herb store in downtown Boulder. Susan had been a regular customer and Esther had grown friendly with her. It had been plain that she was ill: she was pale and emaciated and wore a scarf over her hair. She bought herbs to prevent nausea and help her sleep.

But Esther had loved to see her coming. She always had a joke to tell in her broad Irish brogue and somehow carried such a vital sense of energy with her that Esther felt revived by her presence.

The last time Esther had seen her, Susan was very tired. It was a foggy winter day. They were alone in the fragrant store. As she paid for the small bags of herbs, Susan's hands trembled and Esther had insisted she come sit down to have a cup of hot tea before she left.

Settled by the broad plate-glass window, the gray mist beyond isolating them, Susan had sipped the tea. "I'm ready to go, you know," she said in a matter-of-fact tone.

Esther touched her hand in encouragement. She had learned in her nurses' training that often the best possible thing a nurse could do was let a patient talk. Especially about dying, a subject more taboo than exotic sex.

"I'm not afraid," Susan said, eyeing the pale fog. "It's my husband who can't get past the dying." She smiled at Esther, shaking her head. "You know how men are. They think they can control everything and rage at the heavens in fury when things don't go just as they had planned."

Esther smiled in sympathy, thinking of her father.

"His mother died when he was a teenager and he's never quite overcome the sense of betrayal. I keep hoping he'll get to the point where he can forgive life for taking its capricious turns, but I don't think I can wait much longer."

Still Esther said nothing, just held Susan's hand.

"I got him a cat last week," she said. "It's a horrible animal—should infuriate him enough to keep him going for a while."

Esther chuckled.

"Maybe they'll let me watch over him for a bit," she said with a lift of an eyebrow.

Esther squeezed her fingers gently. "Maybe they will."

Susan's hand tightened in return and she stood up. "I've taken advantage of your good nature," she said and buttoned her coat. At the door, she paused. "Thank you for listening," she said, and left.

Sitting now in the middle of that same woman's room, Esther smiled. Perhaps Susan had been given a guardian job, after all. Stranger things had happened. Thoughtfully she stacked the papers together on the sewing machine. In the yard below, Alexander had finished his series of exercises and simply stood in the grass, staring off toward the mountains, a pensive expression on his face.

Through the joy of loving him, Esther felt a small chill. He had not told her he loved her; not once through the long hours of their lovemaking. He had worshiped her reverently with his hands and lips and eyes; he had given her everything else, but had not confessed to love. As she watched him, he sighed and turned away, his heart obviously heavy.

She loved him. But would even all her love heal the dark scars he carried? Would he let her close enough, or would there come a moment when he shut her out, rather than risk his heart again? Would she be able to prevent it if he decided to lock himself up again in routines and schedules?

A strange urgency gripped her and she turned away from the window and nearly ran down the stairs. He came in the back door as she was coming through the kitchen, and without stopping to think, she rushed forward into his arms, pressing herself against him as if this was her last opportunity.

There was laughter in his voice when he spoke. "Did you miss me so much in so short a time?"

Since she couldn't articulate her sudden fears, she simply nodded.

His arms tightened around her. "Ah, Esther, you are good for my soul." He lifted her chin with one hand. "I can't quite believe my good fortune in finding you."

The words were stated in hushed honesty and his eyes shone with a joy Esther had never seen in them before. Her heart swelled. He loved her, whether he knew it or not, whether he said it aloud or kept it to himself. He loved her.

Golden happiness flooded through her, as warm as the sunlight beginning to pour through the windows.

She smiled as a quickening of desire rippled in her belly. "I'll look forward to this evening," she said.

He gave her a lazy grin as his hands slipped down to curl around her bottom. "So will I." The lightning eyes flashed turquoise. "Already I'm beginning to feel quite vampirish."

The quickening in her belly spread outward as he playfully nipped her neck, and she laughed. "I'd better arm myself with garlic."

"It won't help." Reluctantly he lifted his head. "I'd best go now, before I find it impossible."

Esther couldn't make her wish of an isolated cabin or a ship awash on the Pacific come true. Her days were spent consulting with electricians and carpenters, insurance adjustors and loan officers. Alexander spent his at the university, not only teaching the few summer classes he had, but making preparations for the fall as well.

But the nights came as close to her vision as anything could have. They watched horror and suspense movies, eating popcorn, or sat in the rose-scented garden until very late, talking quietly under a canopy of glistening stars.

And they made love. In the usual places and less usual—on the couch while a movie played forgotten on the VCR, popcorn spilling unnoticed to the floor; in the shower while water ran silkily over their entwined bodies; once against the wall in the kitchen, moments after Alexander came home from work.

It made her blush sometimes to think of it. Both of them seemed a little drunk with passion, drunk enough to disregard anything but the promise of joining one more time. Even now, as she stir-fried green peppers and tomatoes with strips of beef for their supper, she couldn't wait for him to come home so that she could kiss him. He was a wonderful lover— tender and slow at times, furiously passionate at others. She never tired of touching his sleek, hard body or feeling his sensual lips upon her. Liquid heat spilled through her, just thinking of it.

Stirring the mix in the wok, she frowned. Even through the haze of love and hunger, she worried about things a little. While she'd always known that he led an orderly life, she'd not understood just how orderly until she stayed with him. He rose at the dot of seven and went directly outside to go through his tai chi regimen. Afterward, he drank coffee and ate an omelet or bacon and bread for breakfast, then showered and went to work.

In the evenings, he headed directly for the kitchen for a single bottle of ale that he drank in the garden. His world was disciplined.

He liked her children, enjoyed them in ways men often didn't. If given the chance, he would love them. But he had no idea how radically two young boys would change his life. There would be no quiet at seven, no peace at five in the afternoon. The house, while hardly neurotically clean, was generally tidy. Children would change that, too. She grimaced. Not to mention how Esther herself would change it.

As if her thoughts had summoned him, he came into the kitchen. His curls were tousled from the walk home, his broad nose a little sunburned. The tie with its tiny pattern of swords was loose around his neck, his shirt unbuttoned to show a broad triangle of golden chest. "It's hot out there," he said, shoving a hand through the riot of hair. He reached into the fridge for a bottle of ale and frowned as he caught her eye. "Uh-oh," he said. "Looks like Esther's been fretting again."

With a grin, he caught her from behind, an arm around her neck, the other around her waist. "What is it, my sweet?" There was amusement in his voice. "What are you trying to protect me against today?"

She smiled at being pegged so accurately. "The usuals," she admitted.

"If I were you, love," he murmured against her neck, "I'd worry about protecting myself against the vampire that is about to devour you." He bit her neck.

Esther shivered. "Somehow, I keep forgetting that garlic."

"Darn." He rubbed a circle over her stomach, then wickedly over a breast. "Come on, I'll chase those worries away."

And he did.

Alexander was required to attend a faculty dinner the following week, to which he asked Esther to go. She protested she had nothing to wear since the fire had burned her clothes. The next day, he brought a dress home with him—a brilliant blue, with winking rhinestone buttons and a flowing skirt and wide-cut shoulders. She tried it on, but looked so unhappy he took her hand.

"If you don't like it, you can say so. It won't hurt my feelings."

"It's beautiful, Alexander." She sighed. "I just feel really nervous about going with you to something like that."

"Why?" It had never occurred to him that she would be shy in any situation.

"They'll all have advanced degrees and prestigious positions." She lifted one shoulder in a shrug. "I don't belong."

"Ah, so that's it, my silly queen," he said with a grin.

She frowned. "I'm not kidding. I'll feel like the girl from the wrong side of the tracks. They'll ask me what I do and when I tell them, their eyes will glaze over."

"You're the colonel's daughter."

"Oh, yes. And we all know how popular the Army is on college campuses." In her warm brown eyes was the shadow of insecurity that sometimes resided there.

He took her arms. "Esther, they're no more intelligent or well-bred than you are. They'll like you as much as I do."

"They're better educated."

The truth struck him. He inclined his head for a moment thoughtfully, wondering why he hadn't understood it before. He let the subject drop.

But the next day, he picked up an application to the university, financial-aid forms, scholarship information—everything he thought she might need. "Here," he said as he came into the house. "I brought you something."

Esther accepted the sheaf of papers curiously, brushing a stray wisp of hair from her face as she looked at them. Her smile of welcome faded. "What triggered this?" she asked warily.

"You did, yesterday. It's time to quit putting off that dream of yours, Esther. You want your degree, whether or not you know it." He took a bottle of ale from the fridge. Piwacket heard the tip whoosh off, and came trotting into the kitchen, eyes blinking sleepily. When Alexander lifted the bottle and drank with great thirst in the hot afternoon, the cat meowed raggedly and bumped his leg.

Quite suddenly, he realized how Esther's coming had changed his life. He remembered how empty the house had been in the evenings before she'd come to stay with him, how he'd shared his bottle of ale with his cat instead of another human being. As Esther stood now in the middle of the kitchen, her cloud of hair falling forward to hide her face as she stared down at the packet of papers in her hands, his emotions grew very clear. He reached for her hand and lifted it to his lips. "I love having you here," he said.

She raised her head and he read the question in her eyes. Once again, he'd sidestepped expressing himself, but the moment had passed. Although he read the disappointment in her face when he let go of her hand, he found the words still choked him.

"I thought about the dinner," she said. "I'll go with you if you want me to."

He grinned. "I don't want to drag you to an execution or anything."

"No, you aren't." She lifted a shoulder and smiled softly. "I decided you were right. And I'd really like to be with you, wherever you are."

Again his emotions lit and flowed through him. *I love you,* he thought. And he saw the answer in her beautiful face, a radiance he felt honored to have bestowed upon him.

She put the papers aside and hugged him wordlessly, then let him go. "I know you're hot. Go take a shower and I'll fix a salad for us to eat outside."

As he'd known she would, Esther added a rare spirit to the faculty dinner. He watched her all evening, making the small talk she'd been schooled in since toddlerhood, putting people at ease, making them laugh. She glowed in the blue dress that he'd chosen, the simple fabric clinging to her womanly hips and strong legs. More than one man barely concealed his disappointment when she turned her attention to someone else.

He was proud of her and proud to be with her, fiercely so. Watching her across the room, he realized for the first time that he didn't want to let her go back home when the wiring in her house was finished, couldn't bear the thought of his home now without her in it.

He imagined the years ahead, the pleasure of her company easing this sort of gathering. He imagined himself being in the audience when she was awarded her degree, a child on either side of him, all of them cheering as she walked over the stage. He imagined her old, her red hair gone white, pottering around an herb garden.

And yet, he still had not even told her that he loved her. Standing in the company of two associate professors, she laughed at a joke one of them told. The sound rang out, robust and vibrant. Then, as if she felt his eyes, she glanced toward him. Her eyes burned suddenly with a sexy fire, a come-hither somnolence.

Grinning, he let his eyes fall to her mouth and imagined the taste of those ripe pink lips, then his gaze tiptoed over her neck and the demure but enticing swell of her breasts at the bodice of her dress. He caressed her with his eyes, watching her nipples tighten just enough that he knew she was as aroused as he. He looked back to her face and saw the lust in her smile.

To hell with convention. He suddenly wanted her with such power he couldn't breathe. "Excuse me," he said briskly to the man who was telling him about an archaeological dig in Peru that promised miraculous additions to the knowledge of ancient Indian life.

He stalked toward her, took her hand and left the small common room. "Alexander, where are we going?"

"Someplace isolated," he growled. He didn't dare even look at her. They crossed the campus under cover of night, surprising a pair of lovers kissing in an alcove.

In his office, he closed and locked the door. Moonlight streamed in through the window, and he flung it open to let the stuffy air out of the room. He turned back. "Come here," he said.

A slow smile spread over her face as she approached him, a smile that said she knew exactly what they were doing there. It was the last push he needed. He grabbed her and kissed her with a mindless, violent passion. He pushed his hands beneath her dress, his hands skimming up her thighs to her panties. Her mouth opened to him and she loosened his tie, her fingers as eager as his own.

He tugged her panties down as he kissed the valley between her breasts. Esther unfastened his shirt and loosened the confines of his trousers, her tongue hot on his mouth, her teeth digging with barely restrained hunger into his lips, his neck, his chest. He groaned when he found with his hands that she was ready for him, and he settled her on the edge of his desk, reaching around her to push the papers scattered there to the floor. He urgently opened the buttons on her dress and the fastening of her bra, pushing them both away from her gloriously beautiful shoulders. Moonlight cascaded through the window, silvering the curve of her cheek, the pale flesh of her breasts, the long, lovely expanse of her arms.

He drove into her and Esther met him with a muffled cry, wrapping her legs around him and lifting into him, her hips braced on the edge of the desk. He found her mouth and drove there as he drove below, and she met him violently, her nails digging into his flesh.

Alexander had thought he could not want her more than he had already, thought his passion would ebb, that it was impossible to want a woman more than he had already wanted Esther. But now, with her skirt shoved up, her breasts bare in the pagan light, his shirt open around him, he thought if he died now, in this moment, he could not have asked more of life.

She gasped and clutched him, her head falling backward as she quivered in passion. Alexander held her, drove harder and met the truth as he left his body to merge with hers once again.

After a moment, she lifted her head from his shoulder. A haze of pleasure softened her features. His emotions welled up and finally spilled over. He took her face in his hands. "I love you, Esther," he said at last. "Don't go home again. Stay with me, bring your children."

Her dark eyes went wide. "Don't say this now, Alexander. You're drunk with passion."

"Yes." He combed his fingers through the cloud of hair and spoke again, very deliberately. "I love you."

As she had once before, she pressed her fingers to his lips. "Shh."

He'd waited too long, he thought with sorrow. Now she didn't believe him. As he gathered her close, smelling lavender on her shoulders, he thought he would simply have to show her he meant what he said.

"Let's go back to your house," she said as they dressed. "I'll make some chocolate fondue and feed you strawberries."

"Mmm. I can think of a few interesting things to do with chocolate."

She laughed, the sound wicked and warm and inviting. "You're insatiable, Dr. Stone."

He caught her hand. "I'll never have enough of you, Esther."

Her reply was lost in the sound of a violent rapping at his office door. "Esther!" It was Abe's voice, urgent and loud.

Esther's eyes flew to Alexander's. He frowned and switched on a light as she smoothed her dress. She opened the door. "What's wrong, Abe?"

"It's Jeremy," he said without preamble. "He got kicked by a horse. They're flying him to Children's Hospital in Denver."

Alexander froze.

"How bad is it?" Esther asked, her voice remarkably calm.

"Bad," Abe said and licked his lips. "It's his head."

Esther looked over her shoulder at Alexander. "Will you drive me?"

And in spite of the panic suddenly flaring in his nerves, the dread that surrounded him like the fires of hell, he replied quite calmly. "Of course."

Chapter Thirteen

The drive seemed endless, although it was less than thirty miles. Overhead, the moon that had seemed so beautiful only minutes before now seemed to flood the fields with grim, cold light. At the wheel, Alexander was utterly silent, his attention focused on the road ahead. Esther felt his tension as palpably as if it were alive. He didn't speak.

She sat in the passenger seat, twisting her hands together, remembering the night before the children left and her odd sense of dread. Why hadn't she paid attention to that intuition? It had *never* led her wrong. When it told her to check on Jeremy, she always found him in trouble or about to get into it.

As the almost endless skyline of Denver came into view, fear clenched her heart and squeezed. Everything she'd ever learned about head wounds in almost four years of nurses' training came back to her. Concussions, contusions, hemorrhage, skull fractures. A dry, hollow thudding chased the words and their symptoms around in her mind.

Please, she begged silently.

The instant they passed through the hospital doors, however, a steely calm overtook Esther. The familiar sharp scents of ammonia and minty alcohol, the pale green fluorescent lighting and the intermittent growl of the overhead paging system were familiar, somehow welcoming. She approached the admissions desk briskly and located Jeremy, then led Alexander to the elevators. As the doors swooshed closed, she took his hand. His fingers were icy cold. "Are you all right?" she asked.

He gave her a quick nod, his eyes fastened firmly on the numbers over the door.

"Alexander, if you're one of those people who hates hospitals, I'll understand. You don't have to come up with me. I'll be okay."

He still didn't look at her, but his voice was oddly strangled when he spoke. "I want to see him." He finally looked at her, and Esther felt a pang at the bleak gray in his eyes. "Please."

She nodded.

John was hovering near the nurses' station when they came out of the elevators, his face drawn, shoulders hunched. Esther saw that he was struggling with tears. Forgetting Alexander, she rushed forward. "John! Where is he? How bad is it?"

"They've got him down the hall, looking him over," he said brokenly and bent his head. "I don't know. I don't understand all this crap."

"Is he conscious. Is his head bleeding?" She took his hand urgently. "Think."

"He wasn't bleeding," he said, "but he's out cold."

A doctor came toward them, her white coat flapping around her. "Mrs. Lucas?" she asked.

"Yes."

"You can come in and see your son if you like. There isn't much we can do except watch him for the next twenty-four hours."

Esther looked at Alexander and gestured toward him. Grimly, his jaw set, he took her hand. In spite of the rigidness of his grip, she took strength from his presence and nodded toward the doctor. "I'd like to see him."

As they headed toward the room, the doctor explained the injury. "He evidently crawled under a stall and startled one of the horses. It caught him on the top of the skull, but luckily he was on the ground and it wasn't as bad as it could have been." She paused before opening the door, her eyes compassionate. "I want to warn you—"

Esther touched her arm. "I know," she said quietly, and went in.

But all the training in the world didn't make any difference when it was her own son lying beneath a crisp white sheet, face bruised and swollen, eyes black, lip swollen from a secondary injury; not when it was her wild Jeremy with such a pallor over his features who lay so deathly still in the big bed. She stepped forward, feeling the tears finally fill her eyes as she bent to press a gentle kiss to his brown little cheek. "Hi, honey," she whispered. "Mommy's here."

She took his small hand, and brushing away her tears, looked back to the doctor.

"There's no fracture," the doctor said. "No sign of hemorrhage, either. At the moment, we have to treat it like a concussion, but since he hasn't regained consciousness ..." She frowned. "It may be a little more serious."

Esther nodded, her eyes on her son. Contusion was the official word for the concern she saw expressed. The brain swelled from its jostling, sometimes requiring surgery to relieve the pressure. It might lead to convulsions, to learning disabilities, to— "I understand."

"I'll leave you alone, then, for a few minutes."

Alexander stepped forward as the doctor departed, his eyes trained on Jeremy's face. With a hand that visibly trembled, he reached out to trace a gentle line over Jeremy's cheek and jaw. Then, as if he couldn't resist, he bent and placed a kiss on the bruised forehead. "Get well, little one," he said.

Then he stepped back from the bed and looked at Esther. "I'll let you be with him a while," he said. "Perhaps I'll take John down for a cup of coffee. He looked like he needed one."

Gratefully Esther smiled through the tears. "Thank you, Alexander."

He nodded.

The night crawled by, a vast silent night that saw Esther, Alexander and John holding vigil. As the hours passed, there was no change. The rambunctious Jeremy lay unmoving, his eyes closed, his breath soughing in and out.

Somehow, Esther managed to hold on to the sense of calm that had overtaken her the moment she walked through the hospital doors. Except for the small break in her composure upon seeing him the first time, she felt no panic at all. She checked him often, sitting with him as long as the nurses would let her, talking quietly about whatever came to mind in a calm, cheerful voice, all the while holding his hand.

Abe came in toward morning, carrying several of Jeremy's favorite stuffed animals. He settled them in next to the boy. "I knew he'd be upset that he didn't have his blanket," he said. "So I went by and got some of his other stuff."

"Thanks."

Toward morning, John caught Esther as she left Jeremy's room to find a cup of coffee. He was haggard in the harsh fluorescent light and circles of weariness looped around his eyes. "I told Daniel I'd get back as soon as I could. Abe's gonna drive me out there."

"Okay."

He bowed his head. "Esther, I'm so damned sorry. If anything happens to him—" he broke off and swallowed. "I don't think I could ever forgive myself."

"He's going to be okay," Esther said, touching his face. She didn't know that for a fact—no one did. But right now, John needed to believe it. "You can't blame yourself."

"Thanks." He took a breath and blew it out. "I'll send Jeremy's blanket with Abe."

Esther nodded. "I'll call Daniel as soon as I can. He's probably pretty upset."

He rubbed his face. "Better get going, I guess." He started forward, then stopped. "Alexander's a hell of a guy, Esther. I'm real glad for you."

"Thanks."

He wandered away, presumably to find Abe. Esther stood in the middle of the hall for a long time, only startled out of her daze by an orderly carrying a tray. Shaking herself awake, she realized she was extremely tired. Soon she would have to get a little sleep or fall over on her face.

She'd been about to get a cup of coffee. That would help. There was a perpetual pot in the waiting room.

But as she went into the small room, she saw Alexander standing by the window. One elbow was braced on the sill, the other on his hip. A ruddy glow of sunrise washed over him, lending a spirit of joy that was entirely false.

For Esther had never seen such hopelessness in all her life. His back was rigidly erect, his pose casual to the less discerning eye, but with the part of her that had become irretrievably linked to him, she knew.

He had walled himself off. Before he even turned to show her the aching loneliness in his eyes, she knew he was lost to her. When he spoke, his voice was extraordinarily calm. "How is he?"

"About the same," she said abruptly and crossed to the coffee machine in the corner.

"What will happen now?"

She shook her head. "I don't know, Alexander." Not daring to look at him, she opened packets of sugar and cream and dumped them into the paper cup. "Whatever it is, it's going to be a while before we know." She swallowed. "Why don't you go home and get some rest?"

"No." His jaw was rigid. "I'll stay until they know what's next. Maybe then."

A sense of relief rippled through her and she closed her eyes. Maybe he wouldn't shut her out after all. Maybe he'd learned that life never stayed simple or sweet, that it ran a hilly course.

As if he'd heard her thoughts, he quoted quietly, "'A minute to smile and an hour to weep in.'" His voice roughened and he paused, his face still turned toward the sun that rose slowly in the east, throwing sparklers of orange and red over the glass of the buildings below. "'And never a laugh but the moans come double.'" He turned to Esther, raising cynical eyebrows. "'And that is life.'"

"Paul Laurence Dunbar," she said, holding her cup to her lips. "I did a paper on him in college."

The doctor appeared in the doorway. "Mrs. Lucas, Jeremy is stirring."

Both of them hurried after her, and nearly ran to Jeremy's room. A small cry came from his lips when he saw her. "Mommy!"

Esther rushed forward, taking his hand in joy. "I'm here, honey."

His eyes were droopy and swollen, and the pupils were unmatched, but Esther had never seen so beautiful a sight as those deep brown irises, looking at her, seeing her. A joyful rush of tears blurred her vision.

"I'm sorry," he said, his lips turning down. "I climbed the tree."

"It's okay, honey." Gently she smoothed his curls away from his forehead. "It's okay. You just rest now."

Alexander had been standing back, but he stepped forward now to stand next to Esther. He didn't say a word, but Esther saw the relief in his dark blue eyes, saw the trembling in his hands as he touched the small body below the sheets.

Jeremy's eyes had drifted closed again, but at Alexander's touch, he opened them. "Hi," he said.

Alexander smiled. "Shh. You get some sleep now."

"I have a headache," he said, a frown flitting over the bruised brow. But his eyelids drifted down again.

The doctor nodded at them and they left him alone again. In the hallway, Alexander said, "Why did he say that about the tree?"

"He probably won't remember about the horses. Just that he hurt himself. Since I made a big impression with the cantaloupe and the tree, he probably put that in the hole."

Suddenly she was dizzy with relief and exhaustion. "I have to sit down for a few minutes."

For the first time since leaving his office an eternity before, he touched her. He slipped his arm around her shoulders and led her to the waiting room, seeing her settled before he left to find food and juice.

By the time he returned, Esther had come to two conclusions. Jeremy would recover. Alexander would not. His honor would see that he stood by her in this crisis, but his heart was truly buried.

Because for the first time since she'd known him, his touch had carried no current. He'd shut the generator down.

By the time Alexander got home late Friday afternoon, he was grimy with the sweaty worry of the long night and disoriented with a lack of sleep. The bright hot sunlight falling in yellow bands on the porch surprised him oddly. Everything looked just as it should have: a wind had caught the curtain upstairs and pulled it out to flap against the house, Piwacket slept in the shade of a bush, the mountains stood burly guard against the horizon.

And yet, once again, everything had changed.

Wearily he went inside his still house, feeling the emptiness Esther's absence created in its wake. He'd grown used to coming home to find her in the kitchen or kneeling in the garden cutting flowers, had grown used to holding her through the night, her lavender-scented skin warm against his own.

Without bothering to open a bottle of ale or check the cat's food dish, he collapsed in a chair, hearing the silence roar in his ears.

He remembered the last time he had come home from a hospital. A wintery day where this one was hot, and an early dark had closed him inside the house. Then, too, everything had looked just the same. But Susan had breathed her last in the hospital, holding his hand.

Shattered, he'd come home in a daze, unable to gather himself enough to even fix a meal. His hunger had driven him out to find food, and as he'd walked through the crowded streets, he'd been distraught to find the world continued on just as it had before. It didn't come to a screeching halt in stunned horror. The world didn't know, and most of it didn't care, that a single life had passed from its realm.

That night, he had retreated back to the silence of his house where at least the passing was noted.

It had been the same with his mother—the world chattered on its way. Birds didn't fall from the trees, but continued to sing. The sun rose and set as it had for millions upon millions of years. The wind blew, the snow fell.

He groaned, now, fighting the despair he so despised. He wanted to cry like a boy, cry out at the injustice. But as he closed his eyes, he saw Jeremy's pale face, drained of life and energy.

Jeremy, the wild one, the vital one—the one who surged forward heedlessly to meet life with arms outstretched, head flung back. And as if in punishment, life had slapped him down. As it had Susan and Juliette.

Esther. Esther who glowed with vibrance and health and energy enough for ten women, Esther who wept with the fullness life gave her, Esther who dared life to give her everything it had. Even in the midst of the crisis, he'd seen her excitement over being in the hospital, the way she inhaled the acrid scents into her body like perfume. Even under the threat of losing her beloved child, she *dared* to live, almost in defiance.

It terrified him.

As a teenager, grappling with the sudden death of his mother, Alexander had tried to imagine himself as a tree—a young sapling bent almost in half by the fierce winds of life. He'd borne that death, gone on, and in time found Susan. Her death buffeted him once again, breaking limbs of faith and hope.

Last night, the hurricane howl of a threat to Jeremy had chilled his soul. He knew that another great loss would kill him, the way a tornado destroyed the trees in its path.

Until last night, he had not realized that loving Esther meant also risking his heart on her children, that instead of risking the loss of one, he would love and risk three times that number.

He couldn't bear it. The night Esther had told him losing a spouse was not the same as losing a child, he'd thought she simply didn't understand. But it had been he who didn't understand.

For as he'd taken Jeremy's small hand into his own, a thousand bright memories had flitted through his mind. He'd seen the laughing child in the stream, the concentrated scowl of karate practice, seen the little raven cawing on the sidewalk—and his heart had nearly burst. In that i stant, he would have traded his soul for a promise of Jeremy's health.

All the way home, he'd grappled with the dark fear, but nothing assuaged it. Everyone he'd loved had been taken from him. To avoid that loss, he simply could not love.

He could not love.

His recovery was slow, but Jeremy gradually improved. His speech at times slurred somewhat and his emotional state was erratic, veering from hysterical giggling to sharp irritation to vague apathy within hours. Esther stayed with him, sleeping on a cot provided for parents by the hospital. Often Abe or Alexander or Melissa came to relieve her, taking turns reading aloud or watching television or telling him stories. On those breaks, Esther walked outside or went to a nearby café for a solid meal, knowing she had to keep up her strength.

In the meantime, she hurried the electricians by phone, promising a bonus if they could finish their work on time. The carpenters she'd hired were less cooperative, but they, too, finally agreed to finish their repairs by Wednesday. By then, Jeremy would be getting ready to come home. She wanted him in his own environment in order to heal.

Alexander remained distantly friendly with her. She kept half expecting him to take her aside and explain that he needed some time to assimilate the new fear he felt. Another part of her was amazed that he could so completely shut her out after the things they had shared. How could he look at her and not remember the wild passion that had marked these past few weeks? How could he simply walk away from the transcendent beauty of their joining, turn his back on the holiness that had permeated the exchange of their souls?

And yet, even as she wondered, she knew. The control that so marked his mastery of tai chi, the concentration that had seen him through two devastating losses in his life, now served to see that he would not suffer another.

In another time, another place, Esther would have instinctively reached out to try to help him, to try to soothe the virulent pain she sometimes saw in his changeable eyes. Not now. Between meeting her sons' need of her and her own needs, she had nothing left.

One afternoon, Alexander came in a few minutes before supper. Jeremy had drifted off to sleep and Esther smiled. "You just missed him."

He glanced away, then back at her. "I really came to see you today," he said, but the words were so terribly formal Esther heard them with dread.

"All right. Shall we go have a glass of lemonade or something?"

"Actually it won't take long." He touched his beard as if weighing his words, then handed her the papers he carried in his hands. "Watching you the past few days here, I've realized how good a nurse you'll be. I hope you'll give serious thought to completing your degree."

Esther looked at the sheaf of forms and smiled. "When you gave these to me the first time, I was terrified," she said quietly, then looked at him. "But now I know how much I've missed—" she waved to the room, encompassing everything "—all of this. As much as I've hated Jeremy being a patient, I've loved having the excuse to be here. I always tell the children that they should do what they love when they grow up. It's time I took my own advice."

"Good for you, Esther." His eyes softened momentarily, then shuttered tight once more. He swallowed. "There's something else I want to say."

Her heart plummeted. "Don't. Let's just let it go." She bit her lip as tears threatened to choke her. "I've loved being with you, Alexander, but I really do understand."

For a long, long moment, he simply looked at her across the room and Esther saw it all—the love he held for not only her, but for her children; the joy he'd known, the bleakness that had once again stolen the joy away. Then it was gone, and his eyes shone an opaque, even blue with no flicker of silver or turquoise or anything else. "I'm sorry, Esther."

"I'm not."

There was nothing else to say then, and he turned to go. "I have you scheduled for one more class—this coming Thursday. I'll wrap up the lecture for you, shall I?"

"No, Alexander, I think I'd like to do it myself."

He nodded. "I'll see you then."

For the last time. It was unspoken, but very clear.

Chapter Fourteen

By some miracle, the electricians finished their job on Monday and Esther was able to bring Jeremy home on Tuesday. The carpenters still had a few loose ends to finish off, but it was nothing they couldn't do with people in the house.

The smell of fresh lumber hung in the rooms, and after getting her son settled on the couch with his electronic piano, Esther went around admiring the new outlets and fixtures that had been installed. She'd always loved the old-fashioned push-button light switches, but even the loss of them didn't mar her swelling pride. The house had been saved. As far as she was concerned, that was quite an accomplishment.

John brought Daniel home that same night, and as her eldest came up the walk, his dark hair shining,

Esther burst out of the house to pick him up. "Oh, I missed you," she whispered.

"Where's Jeremy?" he asked anxiously. "I thought he came home from the hospital." In his hands was a package wrapped in Sesame Street paper, fastened with an excess of tape.

"He's right inside, sweetie."

Daniel jumped up the porch steps, Esther and John following behind.

"Hi, Jer," Daniel said quietly. "How are you?"

"Fine. Look at my black eyes!" He opened his lids exaggeratedly wide.

"Wow." Daniel murmured in the same tone an adult would have used to let a child know how wonderful he thought he was.

"You should have seen them before," Jeremy said with the air of one who's lived an extraordinary amount. "They were real bad, huh, Mommy?"

"Pretty bad," Esther agreed.

Daniel thrust the package at his brother. "I got you a get well present. I picked it out myself."

Jeremy tore open the paper and chortled with glee at the enclosed gift—a set of electronic drumsticks. "All right! Now we can play together!"

"Oh, boy," Esther said dryly, with a sidelong look at her former husband.

"I swear, Daniel picked them out. I had nothing to do with it."

She glanced back to the faces of her children. Both were radiant, Daniel's with the pride of having picked the right gift, Jeremy's with being the recipient of such careful, loving attention. As she watched, Daniel rubbed his brother's shoulders lightly, the attentive elder brother.

Her eyes misted dangerously and she waved a hand toward John. "Let's leave them alone for a minute."

In the kitchen, he squatted on the stool, accepting the glass of lemonade she poured for him. "This was pretty hard on Daniel," he said. "He said about a hundred prayers a day for him."

"Poor baby." It occurred to her that Daniel was a lot like Alexander. Both of them were unable to protect themselves against negative emotions—or positive ones for that matter. Swallowing, she pushed the thought of Alexander out of her mind. It was too late for him, but maybe she could prepare her son to face a world that was sometimes harsh.

"Is Jeremy okay now?"

"He'll be fine," she said with a smile. "It'll be a few weeks before he can try to kill himself again, but there won't be any permanent damage."

John frowned and laced his fingers around his lemonade glass. "Esther, I've always liked the way you raised these boys, but the next time that child does something around me to nearly kill himself, I will blister his little behind till he can't sit down." He rubbed his face. "Lost ten years of my life when I saw him in that stall."

"I know," she said quietly. "We'll work it out. We'll teach him." She turned away, ostensibly putting the lemonade back into the fridge, but really gathering her courage. "John, there's something I want to talk to you about."

"What? Are you gettin' married?"

She couldn't quell the quick surge of pain that sliced through her at his words. A small voice in her heart cried the name of the man who had given her back her dream, and she looked at her hands. "No," she said softly, then looked at him. "I'm going to finish my nursing degree. Jeremy will be in school in the fall, and I'll have time."

He nodded, waiting for her to continue.

"What I need from you is time, John. I need your help with the children."

"What are you gonna do about the store?"

"I've thought about that, too. I'm going to ask Abe if he'd like to live here—rent free—and tend the store while I'm in class. He's really been much happier since he started working here."

John lifted his glass and drank before he spoke. "I've always felt bad about your degree, Esther. I'll do whatever I can."

She hugged him impulsively. "Thank you."

"You're welcome, Esther." A rare huskiness touched his voice, but he untangled himself quickly. "Don't get all mushy, now. I'm just returning the favor."

"Okay," she said with a laugh.

As she saw him out, she was grateful for their friendship, for her children, for her new wiring, for her renewed dream.

Why then, did she feel so lost?

When Abe came in the following day to help her return the store to order, he was gray and wan. Esther took one alarmed look at his face and sat him down on a chair, rushing to fix a cup of restorative tea. "You have no business being out today," she said.

"I threw my back out, Esther," he said with annoyance. "It's not like I've got some dread disease or anything." He rubbed the spot. "Not like Alexander."

She swallowed, her hands frozen on the cup. "What do you mean?"

He narrowed his eyes. "Don't play dumb with me, Esther Lucas. I've known you for twenty years or better."

"I haven't seen him in several days, for your information. How could I know what's wrong with him?"

"You know." He glared at her. "You're the one who broke his heart."

"I'm the one!" She slammed the mug down on the table, jarring spoons in a basket. "He's the one that walked away from me, not the other way around."

Abe shook his head. "I watched you both in the hospital that night. He was torn to shreds by what happened to Jeremy, and you plain wouldn't look at him."

"I had a child who needed me."

"Not as bad as a certain man did." He looked at her hard. "You're just so sure you don't deserve something good that you went out of your way to let him go."

A surge of fury swept through her—the blinding anger of someone who doesn't get angry often. "You have some nerve, Mr. Smith. You played matchmaker with me, without my permission, with a man who had the kind of wounds you knew I wanted to avoid."

She stepped forward, pointing at him with a finger. "You knew I didn't want that, you knew I had a history of being the fix-it lady. And you brought me Alexander."

"And you fell in love," he said quietly.

Esther bit her lip. "Yes." The word was a whisper.

He reached for her hand. "Esther, he loves you, too. You can't just give up like this. It's such a waste."

Firmly Esther shook her head. "Abe, I can't heal him. Only he has that power."

"I agree with you. You can't be the fix-it lady, but you can let him know you're there for him."

A flare of hope, orange against the sorrow of the past few days, soared through her. But cautiously, she shook her head. "I don't know. We'll just have to see."

But somehow, his words lingered. After supper, the children brought coloring books outside while she did some long-neglected weeding in the herb garden. Their voices reached her, sweet and reassuring as she knelt amid the lavender, plucking stubborn dandelions from between the roots. The heady scent of the flowering lavender filled her nostrils and reached through her defenses to dissolve the barriers she'd erected against thoughts of Alexander. Since the night in the herb garden, the pungent scent had always made her think of him.

Now as her hands brushed the aromatic leaves, she let him flow into her mind, whole and complete. Abe said she needed to let him know she was there for him. Perhaps she did.

But he had to understand she could promise nothing. There were no promises in life. No guarantees of happiness or eternal bliss.

Rocking back on her heels, she looked at her children. Suddenly she remembered when she'd finally gotten a handle on the problems of mortality herself. A smile of inspiration bloomed on her face. There was one class lecture left. Perhaps she could give Alexander a key to opening the rest of his life.

And for once, she wasn't thinking like a healer, but like a queen whose king thought the kingdom had fallen. Somehow, she had to find a way to make him see that it was only a trick of the light that made him think so.

Alexander stood nervously in his classroom Thursday morning, wondering if his armor would hold up when Esther appeared. A handful of students drifted in, laughing among themselves, and then a few more. Another one, by himself. No Esther.

Five minutes after class officially began, he glanced at his watch once more and frowned. "I thought Ms. Lucas would be here to finish her series, but it looks as if she's been detained." A gut-wrenching clutch of disappointment struck him, but he covered it by consulting his notes. "In her absence, I'll finish my own series."

"No, I'm here," came a breathless voice behind him.

He turned, bracing himself, adjusting his mental armor. "Good," he said, his voice remarkably calm.

And then he looked at her. Her pale red hair was loose around her porcelain face, her cheeks flushed.

She smiled briefly at him, as if there had never been anything but a casual friendship between them, then turned toward the class. "Sorry I'm late, everyone," she said and settled one hip against the desk at the front of the class. "Let's get started."

Alexander walked to the back of the room and instead of taking his usual seat, leaned against the wall. She wore her damned yellow blouse, the first thing he'd ever seen her in. The pale expanse of exposed shoulders seemed to glow with an inner source of pearlescent light. He found himself devouring the swell of her breasts, the sensual roundness of her arms, the lush curve of her hips.

With a flash of accursed heat, he recalled in vivid detail how her throat had tasted beneath his tongue, how beautifully pagan she had been the night in his office with the moon floating over her naked breasts like a silver scarf.

He turned away, looking out the window while she talked.

"I won't take long today," she said. "We've covered almost everything I know about medicine in the dark ages, and I think you've received a suitably gloomy picture."

An appreciative laugh met her words.

"Today I think I want to share an angle of life in those bygone days that we could learn from now, an attitude that stemmed directly from the harsh reality those people faced day in and day out."

Listening, Alexander tautened, sensing her next words would be directed at him. It took everything he had to keep himself from turning back to listen, but he thought again of the bleakness that so tormented him and hardened his resolve.

"Modern people," she said, "expect guarantees in everything. And when life doesn't conform to their demands for perfection, they sue doctors and hospitals and look for someone to blame. People spend years in bitter fights with the courts, trying to fix blame for things there is no answer for."

Alexander turned, narrowing his eyes. A hard thudding in his chest made him feel light-headed. And still she didn't look at him.

"I've recently been through a harrowing experience with one of my children, and it reminded me of my own wish, once upon a time, that I could get a guarantee." She paused, her hands folded in her lap. "Not many of you probably have children, but let me tell you, a baby is one of the smallest, most helpless creatures you will ever encounter. I'd been studying nursing when my first child was born, and I knew every possible disease and injury that could happen to him." She grinned ruefully. "I was a wreck, wondering how I could possibly survive if something happened to him—and it seemed like almost anything could happen. So, I had another baby—just in case."

Her expression sobered. "It didn't help. My love and my worries were just doubled. It seemed dangerous to love anything as much as I loved those two tiny, helpless babies."

Alexander felt his throat tighten until he could barely breathe.

"One afternoon, I was driving on the highway with my new baby and his slightly older brother. And a truckload of construction workers drove by. They all started whooping and hollering," she said dryly, and looked at some of the women in class with a raised eyebrow. "You know what I mean."

Laughter rippled through the room.

"Anyway, I looked at all those big, strong men who looked as if a falling tree couldn't hurt them and I realized that every single one of them had once been a baby."

Still she didn't look at Alexander. "It's a miracle that any of us are even conceived, much less grow up and grow old. In the dark ages, they survived by remembering that miracle of each and every day. They survived in spite of horrors we can't even contemplate now by meeting each day as it came and celebrating the turn of the seasons with festivals and feasts."

Finally she lifted her serious brown eyes to Alexander's face. "As far as I'm concerned, that was the best medicine they could have had—and it probably beats the heck out of a lot of things we have now."

She stood up. "It's been great, guys. Good luck." With a swirl of her paisley skirt, she walked out.

It had been an hour since Esther had left his class, and Alexander's hands were still shaking. Her lecture had not been directed to the class, but to him.

God help him, but he missed her. He missed the children and the noise, missed her clutter. He wanted her so fiercely he thought of almost nothing else. Everywhere he went, everything he did echoed with Esther's imprint.

So now, in the high noon of a Colorado mountain summer, he walked. Through parks and streets, past shops and restaurants, through business districts and residential settlements. Walked until his legs ached.

He walked until he stood beside Susan's grave. He stared at the gray headstone for a long time, trying to bring her face alive in his mind. Instead he saw Esther's and Daniel's and Jeremy's.

As if echoing his mood, a bank of dark clouds had gathered over the mountains, and a gust of wind swept through the graveyard, kicking up leaves and old flowers. He blinked.

What if it were Esther, lying here below the cold earth? Or Jeremy or Daniel?

What if?

A pigeon cooed mournfully. The wind gusted. And a soft, gentle rain began to pour from the sky—a rarity in this land of quick, brutal storms.

Alexander didn't move as it dampened his shirt and hair. It was a warm rain and he closed his eyes, lifting his face to the life-giving water, feeling it pool and spill over his cheeks. It trickled over his scalp and wet his neck and still he stood there, head thrown back.

Feeling it.

What if nothing happened to any of them? What if Esther and Daniel and Jeremy all lived to be ninety?

He straightened abruptly. And as if Susan was a ghost, he saw her clearly in the gray rain, laughing at his foolishness. In memory, he heard her voice: *You'll be sorry at the end of your days, Alexander.*

And with incredible, blinding clarity, he realized Susan had had no regrets. She had gone to her grave much too soon, but on that grim cold winter day four years before, she had bid farewell to a life that had been worth bidding farewell to.

He thought of Esther in her kitchen after their day in the mountains, fingering her purple coleus with an air of wonder, tears rolling out of her eyes. He'd asked her if there was anything wrong.

She'd raised her fabulous brown eyes and said, "I'm just too full."

As he had been these past months with joy and humor and love. All he wanted was to return to that circle, to the brilliance of her, to her giggling children and their bustling noise and breathtaking insights.

He looked back at the grave and smiled.

Jeremy was napping upstairs. Abe and Melissa had taken Daniel to a movie. The store was empty. A soft blues ballad played on the alternative radio station. A pattering rain fell against the windows.

Esther wandered out onto the protected porch, crossing her arms over her chest. The world was beautiful when it rained, she thought wistfully. Leaves nodded and shimmered, and the harsh edges of everything were softened.

A figure emerged from the gray: a man, heedless of the rain that had soaked him. Esther's heart squeezed. It was Alexander.

He stood on the sidewalk for a moment, staring at her, his face unreadable. His wild curls defied even the rain's attempts to subdue them and sprung up in disarray over his proud, well-shaped head. The sodden shirt clung to his leanly muscular body and rain trailed in streams from the silvered beard.

Her breath caught. And he started forward, purpose in his step.

At the foot of the stairs, he looked up at her. "I've been to the graveyard," he said.

"Have you?" It was impossible to tell from his expression what he had come to tell her. "And?"

He climbed the steps to the porch and looked down at her for a long moment. Beyond the porch, rain splashed against the spirea bushes and a wind blew fine mist over her face. Esther waited.

"I found myself wondering what I'd be feeling if it were you in that grave."

She nodded slowly, her arms folded protectively over her chest.

His eyes were anything but opaque now—the kaleidoscope irises gleamed with a hundred colors, a thousand. "All I could think about," he continued softly, "was how I'd feel if you lived instead and I let you spend all your days with someone else."

A wild hope fluttered alive in her heart and she looked at him. "And?"

He cocked one eyebrow. "I've been a coward and a fool, Esther." He took her hand. "But I love you and if you think you'd be willing to tutor me, I'd really like to learn to live again."

She looked at him, in wonder and lingering fear. "I'm not the fix-it lady," she said. "I can't heal you of the past, Alexander. I can't even promise you that nothing terrible will happen if you love me—us."

Gravely he smiled. "I know."

Tears, always ready for any emotional moment in her life, sprung to her eyes and Esther relented, throwing her arms around his neck, feeling his wet lips upon her temple, his wet clothes cold against her body. "Oh, Alexander, I've missed you so much."

His hug was rib-cracking. "I've been miserable without you, my love," he growled against her hair. "I want to grow old with you, and watch the children grow and eat strange things and laugh." He lifted his head and took her face in his hands. "No matter how many days it is that we have, I want the rest of mine to be spent with you."

She kissed him. "I love you," she whispered over her tears. "And see what you've done, you made me cry silly tears again."

He chuckled and brushed one away with his thumb. "Not many people remember to cry for joy anymore. It's a wonderful gift." He bent and reverently licked the rain from one bared shoulder, grabbing her closer when her knees weakened. His voice was rumblingly suggestive when he spoke again. "Where are the children?"

She told him.

He chuckled, then took her hand and pulled her inside. He locked the door and turned the sign to Closed and pulled her upstairs. Esther's heart beat a frantic rhythm as she watched him. "What are we doing?" she breathed as he closed her bedroom door.

He shucked his shirt, baring the magnificent chest, then reached for her, pushing the yellow blouse from her body. "Celebrating," he said.

And then, somehow, they were making love, half-dressed, joining once more in silvery light. It was exhilarating and rushed and no less sacred than any other time, but this time he breathed into her ear, over and over, "I love you, Esther."

Afterward, he cradled her close and told her that he'd thought of himself as a tree and how the various disasters of his life had affected him, including Jeremy.

"So I thought, you see," he said, leaning over her, "that I would die. But standing there in the graveyard, I realized I'm old oak now, weathered and wounded, but very strong."

Esther smiled, thinking of her lion and king images of him. Whichever metaphor one used, she thought, it didn't matter. The wounded lion was roaring, the king was safely on his throne, the tree would weather the storms of life.

"I'm sorry, Esther, for having put you through this."

She leaned on his chest, kissing the tangle of hair. "I told you before, I'm a patient woman."

"Well, I'm not a patient man. How quickly can you settle your affairs and marry me?"

"Marry you?"

He grinned, his eyes flashing. "Yes, marry. I'm rather old-fashioned about these things, you see. I don't think it provides a good example for the children if we simply live in sin." He sobered. "Because I don't want to waste another single minute of whatever life we have together, Esther. I want you with me."

Another single minute.

"How about the end of the week, then?" she said.

"Done." He kissed her soundly.

"Mommy!" came a voice from down the hall.

Esther looked at him. "Are you sure that you're ready for this?"

"Yes." His eyes blazed turquoise and blue—but at last the bleak gray was gone.

She grinned. "I'll be back."

"I'll be here."

Chapter Fifteen

Two weeks later, Esther stood in the middle of the room that had belonged to Susan. It had been a hot day and the breeze billowing the curtains outward was cool and welcome.

All the boxes had been gathered and sorted, the closet cleaned out. Esther had scrubbed the hardwood floor to a glowing sheen, washed and rehung the curtains and dusted off the sewing machine. Wryly she glanced at it, wondering if she'd ever use it—domestic talents had never come easily to her. Still, it might come in handy.

The children had been in bed for an hour, and in his study, Alexander was savoring the quiet of boys abed as he did every evening. A creature of habit, her lion, but as long as the routines left time for Esther, she didn't mind. In a little while, she would go downstairs and they would sip tea or cognac, play chess or watch an old movie—then end up, as always, tangled together in his big bed. The thought made her smile.

Piwacket jumped into the room through an open window, landing with an ungraceful thud. She whirled, then frowned at him. "How do you get up here?" she asked him.

He rubbed her ankles, bumping his head against her knees. She smiled and reached down to pat his haunches as she would a dog, then straightened and picked up the last box, intending to carry it downstairs with her when she left.

At the door, she paused, looking back to see if she'd forgotten anything. The room glowed peach and white, emanating the sort of tranquillity she'd imagined so often when she'd seen it from outside. And for just an instant, she was struck with the series of lucky coincidences that had placed her in this room.

A sudden gust of wind tossed the curtain by the sewing machine up and over the table. Esther spied the stack of papers sitting there, which she'd left for Alexander to go through. The hem of the curtain had caught on the corners of the pile and a wind ruffled them, tossing several into the center of the room.

Esther dropped the box and hurried across the room. She could see the photo of Susan on top, the curtain caught on its edge. As she reached out to rescue it, the wind sucked out, dragging the curtain back with it. Esther bumped her hip in an effort to grab the curtain and swore mildly, then rounded the table, seeing the photo floating alone at the end of the curtain. Relieved, she grabbed a handful of fabric to draw it back inside.

At that instant, another gust of wind tore the photo from the hem of the curtain. Esther watched it flutter away, borne high into the trees. She watched, leaning out the window into the night, until it danced out of view.

"Lose something?" Alexander asked as he teasingly swatted her behind.

Bemused, Esther turned. For a moment, she looked at him, frowning a little. If she were a different sort of woman—

Then she smiled and reached up to touch her husband's face. "No," she said quietly. "I found something."

"So did I," he said, his voice husky. He kissed her.

Overflowing with love, Esther threw her arms around him and hugged him, closing her eyes as she thought of the picture fluttering away into the night.

Thank you, she breathed silently. "I love you, Alexander," she said aloud, her heart bursting with joy.

"And I," he said, lifting his head to smile down at her, "love you, Esther Stone."

*   *   *   *   *

COMING NEXT MONTH

AVAILABLE THIS MONTH:

Silhouette Special Edition®

Commencing in May . . .

The stories of the men and women who ride the range, keep the home fires burning and live to love.

Cowboy Country

by Myrna Temte

**For Pete's Sake (#739) - May
Silent Sam's Salvation (#745) - June
Heartbreak Hank (#751) - July**

Where the soul is free and the heart unbound . . . and the good guys still win. Don't miss *For Pete's Sake*, #739, the first of three stories rustled up with love from Silhouette Special Edition.

SEDAW-1R

Summer romance has never been so hot!

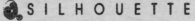

A collection of hot summer reading by three of
Silhouette's hottest authors:

Ann Major
Paula Detmer Riggs
Linda Lael Miller

Put some sizzle into your summer reading. You
won't want to miss your ticket to summer fun—with
the best summer reading under the sun!

"GET AWAY FROM IT ALL" SWEEPSTAKES

HERE'S HOW THE SWEEPSTAKES WORKS

NO PURCHASE NECESSARY

To enter each drawing, complete the appropriate Official Entry Form or a 3" by 5" index card by hand-printing your name, address and phone number and the trip destination that the entry is being submitted for (i.e., Caneel Bay, Canyon Ranch or London and the English Countryside) and mailing it to: Get Away From It All Sweepstakes, P.O. Box 1397, Buffalo, New York 14269-1397.

No responsibility is assumed for lost, late or misdirected mail. Entries must be sent separately with first class postage affixed, and be received by: 4/15/92 for the Caneel Bay Vacation Drawing, 5/15/92 for the Canyon Ranch Vacation Drawing and 6/15/92 for the London and the English Countryside Vacation Drawing. Sweepstakes is open to residents of the U.S. (except Puerto Rico) and Canada, 21 years of age or older as of 5/31/92.

For complete rules send a self-addressed, stamped (WA residents need not affix return postage) envelope to: Get Away From It All Sweepstakes, P.O. Box 4892, Blair, NE 68009.

© 1992 HARLEQUIN ENTERPRISES LTD.   SWP-RLS

"GET AWAY FROM IT ALL"

Brand-new Subscribers-Only Sweepstakes

OFFICIAL ENTRY FORM

This entry must be received by: May 15, 1992
This month's winner will be notified by: May 31, 1992
Trip must be taken between: June 30, 1992—June 30, 1993

YES, I want to win the Canyon Ranch vacation for two. I
understand the prize includes round-trip airfare and the two
additional prizes revealed in the BONUS PRIZES insert.

Name _____

Address _____

City _____

State/Prov. _____ Zip/Postal Code _____

Daytime phone number _____
(Area Code)

Return entries with invoice in envelope provided. Each book in this shipment has two
entry coupons — and the more coupons you enter, the better your chances of winning!
© 1992 HARLEQUIN ENTERPRISES LTD.   2M-CPN

"GET AWAY FROM IT ALL"

Brand-new Subscribers-Only Sweepstakes

OFFICIAL ENTRY FORM

This entry must be received by: May 15, 1992
This month's winner will be notified by: May 31, 1992
Trip must be taken between: June 30, 1992—June 30, 1993

YES, I want to win the Canyon Ranch vacation for two. I
understand the prize includes round-trip airfare and the two
additional prizes revealed in the BONUS PRIZES insert.

Name _____

Address _____

City _____

State/Prov. _____ Zip/Postal Code _____

Daytime phone number _____
(Area Code)

Return entries with invoice in envelope provided. Each book in this shipment has two
entry coupons — and the more coupons you enter, the better your chances of winning!
© 1992 HARLEQUIN ENTERPRISES LTD.   2M-CPN